THE
BEST
MAN

RICHARD PECK

DIAL BOOKS FOR YOUNG READERS

ALSO BY RICHARD PECK

— ✳ ✳ ✳ —

Novels for Young Adults

Novels for Adults

Short Stories

Picture Book

Nonfiction

THE
BEST MAN

DIAL BOOKS FOR YOUNG READERS
PENGUIN YOUNG READERS GROUP
An imprint of Penguin Random House LLC
375 Hudson Street
New York, NY 10014

Library of Congress Cataloging-in-Publication Data

Names: Peck, Richard, date, author.
Title: The best man / Richard Peck.
Description: New York, NY : Dial Books for Young Readers, [2016] | Summary:
"Archer has four important role models in his life—his dad, his
grandfather, his uncle Paul, and his favorite teacher, Mr. McLeod. When
Uncle Paul and Mr. McLeod get married, Archer's sixth-grade year becomes
one he'll never forget"— Provided by publisher.
Identifiers: LCCN 2015049803 | ISBN 9780803738393 (hardback)
Subjects: | CYAC: Family life—Fiction. | Schools—Fiction. | Role
models—Fiction. | Weddings—Fiction. | Gays—Fiction. | BISAC: JUVENILE
FICTION / Family / General (see also headings under Social Issues). |
JUVENILE FICTION / School & Education.
Classification: LCC PZ7.P338 Bes 2016 | DDC [Fic]—dc23 LC record available at
https://lccn.loc.gov/2015049803

Printed in the United States of America
3 5 7 9 10 8 6 4

Design by Mina Chung · Text set in Perrywood

For Lin Oliver

1

Boys aren't too interested in weddings. Girls like them. Grown-ups like them. But my first-grade year started with one wedding, and my sixth ended with another. Call my story "A Tale of Two Weddings." I was in both of them.

One of the weddings was great. In fact, it's just over. There's still some cake. And I got a fantastic new suit out of it. The pants are cuffed. The coat gives me shoulders, and I'll be sorry to outgrow it. I won't mind being taller, but I'll miss the suit.

Also, a pair of gold cuff links are involved, but we'll come to them later.

The other wedding, the first one, was a train

wreck, so let's get that one out of the way. Besides, it happened when I was too little to know what was happening or to stand up for my rights. I didn't have any rights. I was six.

Did I even know what weddings are? And this one wasn't even anybody in our family.

"Archer, honey," said Mom one day. I was in her office for some reason I didn't see coming. Mom's maiden name was Archer. I'm named for her kid brother, Paul Archer.

Mom was about to pull me onto her lap. But I held up both hands. They were red and black with touch-up paint. I was paint all over. I'd sat in some. Dad and I had been out in the garage detailing a vintage '56 Chevy Bel Air.

Mom pulled back, but only a little. "There's going to be a wedding, and guess what? You get to be in it."

"Get Holly," I said. Holly's my sister, seven years older, so she'd have been thirteen or so.

"We already have Holly," Mom said. "She's going to be a junior bridesmaid. She's tickled pink."

"What's left?"

"Ring bearer," Mom said.

"What's that?"

"You carry the bride's ring down the aisle on a little satin pillow."

"Whoa," I said.

"You won't be alone," Mom said. "Don't worry about that. There'll be another ring bearer. She'll carry the groom's ring."

She?

"A darling little girl named Lynette Stanley."

A girl?

"Her mother and I went to college together. We were best buds in the Tri Delt House. The Stanleys have moved here for the schools, so you and Lynette will be starting first grade together, and you'll already be friends!" Mom beamed.

How could I be friends with a girl? I stood there, waiting to wake up from this bad dream.

"I can wear my regular clothes," I said. "Right?"

"Archer, honey, you don't have regular clothes," Mom said. "And by the way, racing-stripe paint doesn't come out in the wash. I suppose your dad's in about the same condition."

"Pretty much," I said.

"We'll look at what you'll wear for the wedding a little later on." Mom glanced away. "A little closer to the event."

I racked my six-year-old brain. There had to be a way out of this. There's always a way out when you're six, right? "Who are they, these people getting married?"

Mom was looking away, far, far away. "The bride is Mrs. Ridgley's granddaughter," she said.

"Who's Mrs. Ridgley?"

"An old friend of your grandmother Magill."

"Were they best buds in the Tri Delt House?"

"No," Mom said. "They were best buds at the Salem witch trials."

2

Every hot August day brought the wedding closer. My sister, Holly, came home from camp and pounded up to her room to try on her junior bridesmaid dress. She about wore it out before the day came. But the day came.

So did my ring-bearer rig, my first FedEx delivery. Mrs. Addison Magill had sent for it—Grandma. I couldn't read, but I knew that much. "Archer," Mom said, "whatever it is, you'll have to wear it. I do my best with your grandmother Magill, but it's never good enough. Never. Be a brave boy."

It was going to be a simple porch wedding, Grandma's porch. They wouldn't even need a rehearsal, which was fine with me. I didn't know what a rehearsal was. Just a gathering of friends. No fuss.

But a hundred and twenty-five chairs were set up on the front lawn when the wedding day dawned. We live behind my grandparents. Two big square houses. Grandpa Magill built them.

Dad stayed down in the garage as long as he could. But time ran out for him too.

"A tie?" I heard him say to Mom up in their room. "I have to wear a *tie*?"

I crouched at the end of my bed. I couldn't sit all the way down in my ring-bearer's rig.

An idea hit me—the best idea I'd ever had in my life. I'd go hide, and after a while they'd forget about me. They might even forget they'd ever had me. Then after the wedding, when the rings were on the fingers, I'd pop out, and they'd all be glad to see me.

I know. A few months older—a few weeks—and I'd have seen all the bugs in this plan. The first thing you learn in school is that there's no place to hide.

I vanished while the coast was clear. Not easy in those shoes. Even the soles seemed to be patent leather. I skidded past Holly's room. And Mom and Dad's, where Mom was tying Dad's tie. Then I was outdoors and across the alley to Grandpa and

Grandma's. August sun glinted off me. I was all in white like the bride.

I came across Grandpa Magill, in the porch swing Dad had set up for him in our backyard. He wore his seersucker suit and a straw hat, and was sound asleep. Cleo the cat was in his lap. She glanced up at me, then stared. Even to the cat I looked ridiculous. Up at the back of Grandma and Grandpa's house, uniformed people were putting glasses on trays. The wedding cake stood under a plastic sheet. I wouldn't have said no to a piece of cake, but I had some disappearing to do.

Now I was moving from one snowball bush to the next, along the side of the house, and the front porch. I slid back a piece of loose latticework down low and slipped inside. Now you see me, now you don't.

I'd been down here under the porch before, making a fort, messing around. It's a cool, webby place with some mud. I was inches from the wedding, but totally invisible.

Footsteps thundered on the porch floor above. Murmuring came from the folding chairs in the yard. A string quartet tuned up directly over my head. Then I got a big surprise.

A face appeared in the open space I'd come

through. I jumped, and cracked my head on a beam. A girl ducked inside. She had a mop of red hair with a big pink bow in it. You could just stand up in here, if you were six. She was a little bigger than I was, all the way around.

Her skirt was a lot of peachy pink net. We seemed to be wearing matching shoes. "Hey, bozo, you're supposed to be *on* the porch, not under it," the girl said. "What are you, five?"

It was Lynette Stanley, of course.

"How'd you know I was down here?"

"I saw you from the living room window." She jerked a thumb over her shoulder. Her dress had weird puffy sleeves.

"Who could miss you in all that white? You look like a snow cone."

It was dim down here, but Lynette Stanley got a good look at me.

"White velvet shorts?" she said. "What were they thinking?"

"Shut up," I said, hopeless.

"They're really tight on you."

Tighter than she knew. I couldn't sit down.

"They're like toddler's shorts," Lynette said. "It's like you wear training pants underneath."

I wasn't wearing anything underneath. How could I? And I was beginning to chafe.

"It's like you drink out of a sippy cup. And look at your shirt. You've got more ruffles down your front than I do."

She held out her skirt. "And I look like Fancy Nancy."

Her dress was a lot of net, a lot of sash, those ruffles. Dorky. She'd had a FedEx delivery too. Above us the string quartet went into "You Are the Wind Beneath My Wings."

"It's a bad dress," I told Lynette, "but you'll be safe down here."

"Are you nuts?" she said. "We're already late. They'll be panicking. They'll be on their phones. It'll be an Amber Alert."

"I'm not going." I put my hands behind me. "You go ahead."

Lynette sighed and made a grab for me. She was planning to frog-march me out from under the porch or something. I jumped back. My slick shoes shot out from under me. I sat down hard, and my hands slapped mud. We heard the sound of stitches popping.

"Whoops," said Lynette.

Something inside me had known this wasn't going to work. A sob started up, behind the baby-blue velvet bow tie.

We were outside now, breezing past the snowball bushes. She'd yanked me to my feet. My hands were muddy, so now *her* hands were muddy. I felt cold slime where I sat.

"They're going to kill me," I said.

"They'll have to get past me first," Lynette said.

She still had me in a grip all the way into the house. Bridesmaids were rustling around in there. They'd already been assigned their bouquets. I guess the bride was still upstairs. There aren't any small weddings. There's always fuss.

Mom in a new dress swooped down on me. "Archer, where . . ." Then she really saw me. "Oh, Archer," she said. "Why?"

Lynette turned me loose. I didn't want to get mud on Mom, so I wiped my hands on my ruffles.

"I did it," Lynette said. "I pushed him in the mud."

Then another woman loomed up, redheaded. She was already spitting on a Kleenex, so she'd be Lynette's mom. "Put out your hands, Lynette. We've got to get the worst of that mud off them," said Mrs. Stanley. "You have to carry a white satin pillow. *Hands,* Lynette."

Lynette turned them up. "This kid—Archer—said my dress was bad and an ugly color, so I popped him one, and he fell in the mud," Lynette confessed. "Went down like a tree."

This was a lie. You were there. You heard. Lynette said it to save me. I couldn't believe it, but I took a hand back from Mom and rubbed my chin as if Lynette had popped me one.

Then here came Grandma Magill. For one thing, Lynette and I had tracked in mud, which you better never do.

Mom was bending over me. She looked up at Grandma. "Hazel, I don't think I can get him cleaned up in time."

Hope flickered in me, for a second or two.

Grandma looked me over. But she didn't see the worst. That was all behind me where I'd sat in the mud. A cool breeze blew back there, into the split in my velvet shorts. A split turning into a gap. Remember—no underpants.

The wedding was running late. Time enough

for the groom to have second thoughts, as Grandma often said later. She gave me one of her looks. An orchid was planted on her big shoulder.

"He goes down the aisle," she said, "just like that." Grandma turned to the front window, scattering bridesmaids. The string quartet was sitting there, holding their bows.

Grandma leaned out the window. "Hit it," she told them.

Holly went first. Her dress looked a little tired, but she was really happy. She'd never worn lipstick this near Mom before. The string quartet was about to go into "Here Comes the Bride."

When Holly reached the top of the porch steps, Grandma gave me and Lynette shoves through the front door.

We were both carrying little white pillows. "Right foot," Lynette muttered. "No. Try the other one."

I slipped and slid on the slick porch. The rings were sewed to the pillows, so that was okay. But now came the stairs.

You never saw that many people in a front yard. The minister was practically out in the street, along with the groom and the best man. You could barely make them out.

Lynette went down a step. I couldn't. My shorts had me in a hammer lock. They were like the jaws of death. I tried it sideways. Nothing. My patent leather shoe hung out in space.

I handed off my pillow to Lynette. I'd have to crawl on all fours, backward. The first bridesmaid was in the doorway, twitching her bouquet.

I started crawling down, bottom high in the August afternoon. With two hundred and fifty eyes on me from the yard. The cameras were already coming out.

There was no seat in my pants now. Only me, muddy and open to the world.

Laughter rippled across the yard. All the cameras were out. I was facing the other way, but I could feel the flash. Lynette, with both pillows, kept even with me.

A year or so later we made it to the foot of the stairs. I was *this close* to bawling.

"Don't," Lynette said, and handed me my pillow.

An old lady sat in the first row with her hand over her eyes. That would be Mrs. Ridgley.

We set off. "Right foot," muttered Lynette, "left foot."

The bridesmaids were coming down off the porch behind us, and here came the bride. But I'd already stolen the show.

Cameras still flashed behind me when the wedding party pulled up out by the street. I was still being uploaded. And Lynette and I were right there till we had to hand over the rings.

Then out of the crowd Dad appeared, in a tie. He swooped down on me and slung me over his shoulder. And off we went to the garage to hide out until this whole wedding blew over. We played Angry Birds, Dad and I. Angry Birds Star Wars, his favorite. SpongeBob Jelly Puzzle 3, mine. We passed on the wedding cake.

So that's how Lynette Stanley and I started. She was bossy then. She's bossy now. But she took the rap for me by saying she'd knocked me in the mud. "You saved my butt," I still tell her.

"Actually, I didn't," Lynette says. "Your six-year-old butt is still on YouTube."

3

Grandpa Magill walked me to the first day of first grade. We started early. He was up before the sun every morning, year-round, waiting for the day to get going. Always in coat and tie and pants with a crease. In the summer he wore his straw hat. On World Series week he always wore his Chicago Cubs cap, even though the Cubs hadn't gone to the Series since 1945 and hadn't won one since 1908.

On the way to school, Grandpa scoped out every house. "See those three in a row? I built them."

He had big knuckles, like a carpenter.

And he acted like he owned all the houses he ever

built. He'd grumble if people put on an addition or enclosed a porch. You wouldn't want to hear what he called aluminum siding. And he wouldn't put up with litter on the lawn.

He turned me loose twice to run a newspaper out of the shrubbery and up to some stranger's door. He kept me so busy I forgot to be scared. Then school loomed up. Kids and their grown-ups were coming from all directions. But on that first day you don't think about anybody but you.

On the school steps, I glanced back for one last look at the world.

Out there, rumbling along the curb, was a '56 Chevy Bel Air. It was detailed to death with red and black flames painted from front bumper to the dual exhausts. A pair of giant fluffy dice dangled from the rearview mirror. It was Dad, shadowing us in the Chevy, making sure Grandpa and I made it to school.

Inside past the security guard, everybody was yelling. Sixth graders were throwing stuff—sandwich parts, whatever.

Grandpa blazed a trail through them. He swung me around a couple of corners, and we pulled up in front of a classroom.

A smiling lady in a corduroy skirt stood there.

Grandpa told her I was his grandson. His hat was off. He waited till I reached up to shake the teacher's hand.

She was Mrs. Bird, and she checked me off a printout, so there was no going back.

I was trying to figure out how Grandpa knew where first grade was when Mrs. Bird gave him another look. "Sir, are you Mr. Addison Magill?"

Grandpa nodded a little bow.

"What an honor to meet the architect of Westside Elementary. I had no idea you were still—I mean, what a pleasure!"

No wonder Grandpa knew where the first-grade room was. It was where he'd put it. He wasn't a carpenter. He was the architect. This was a lot to learn before school even started.

Grandpa gave me a little boost on my backpack. Then he was gone. Now you see him, now you don't.

We began Mrs. Bird's first grade in a circle on the floor, holding our ankles. And guess who was sitting next to me? The new girl with all the red hair. Lynette Stanley.

"Why are you sitting next to me?" I asked, not moving my lips.

"You're the only one here I know."

The Stanleys were new in town. I'd gone to kindergarten with everybody else. All seven boys named Josh were here. Josh Hunnicutt had been the smallest kid in kindergarten and still was. And that meant I wasn't. Russell Beale was back. We'd heard he'd flunked kindergarten and had to repeat it. But it was only a rumor.

It was your regular first grade. Three people were crying. There were a few thumb-suckers. One kid was in some kind of superhero costume with a cape. Two girls had brought their Madame Alexander dolls. The security guard had taken a knife off Jackson Showalter. He'd brought a hunting knife in his backpack to the first day of school.

"Is that the kid they had to disarm?" Lynette nodded across the circle at Jackson. It wasn't nine o'clock yet, and he was famous already. I nodded back. There were missing teeth in every mouth around the circle, but Jackson looked like he'd lost his in a fight.

"And who have I got on my other side?" Lynette said in my ear. I looked.

"Natalie Schuster," I muttered.

Lynette crossed her eyes and held her nose. "She's wearing perfume."

"She could read before kindergarten," I explained. "Books without pictures. She thinks she's a grown-up."

"Weird," Lynette said. "Spooky."

"You think you're a grown-up too," I told her.

"No, I don't," Lynette said. "I've got a fifth-grade vocabulary, but I'm in first."

"Can you read?"

"Isn't that what first grade's *for*?" she said.

Now the teacher was settling on a small chair. She tucked her corduroy skirt. "Boys and girls, my name is Mrs. Bird, so you are my little birds."

Natalie groaned and poked two fingers down her throat.

"Who knows a good word for a little bird?" Mrs. Bird asked.

"Chick," said Natalie. "Birdy. Something like that." Natalie was always first with an answer. She never had to think about it.

"Fledgling," Lynette said.

Mrs. Bird looked really happy. "Fledgling! That's a very good word. That's a fifth-grade word, Lynette."

We had name tags pinned on our shirts.

"Except it's not a word," Natalie said into Lynette's other ear.

Lynette turned to her. "*Fledgling*'s a word."

"No, it happens not to be," Natalie said. "If it was, I'd know it. I was reading before kindergarten. I've read every one of the American Girl books. They ought to write one about me. And I hate your hair."

And so our journey through grade school began. It was already happening in that first circle of Mrs. Bird's fledglings.

In grade school, your best friend better never be a girl unless you *are* a girl. But there sat Lynette Stanley with hardly any space between us, talking my ear off. And when people began to notice we were best friends, I might just as well put on a dress and throw myself backward off the monkey bars.

And there on Lynette's other side was Natalie Schuster. And Lynette had already crossed her. *Teachers* didn't cross Natalie. Even the kindergarten teacher's aide hadn't crossed her.

"Is she going to give me trouble?" Lynette asked me before the circle broke up.

"Maybe, maybe not. Just don't throw around too many big words where she can hear."

And across the circle was Jackson Showalter, hunkered down and blowing his nose with his thumb. He had trouble written all over him, along with a lot of stuff inked on his arms. His shifty eyes scanned the circle.

"Just do me one favor," I said to Lynette. "Don't save me."

"From what?"

"From whatever. You know what I mean. Like you did you-know-when. At the wedding."

"Right," Lynette said. "Save yourself."

"Also, later on, when we have phones, you will never text me. Okay?"

"Deal," said Lynette.

And now I was pretty sure Jackson Showalter's narrow eyes were on me, where I sat next to Lynette Stanley, with Natalie Schuster on her other side.

4

Jackson Showalter took eight months to get around to me. Keeping out of his way gave me a busy winter. By now he'd shaved his head and inked a lot more stuff on his arms. Not words. I don't know if he knew any words. By April the rest of us could read, more or less. We were all heading for Captain Underpants and punctuation, except for Jackson, who was heading for me.

I have an April birthday, April 23, which is the date in 1914 when a major-league ball game was first played in Wrigley Field. So it was my birthday, and I made the mistake of wearing my best present to school the next day.

My uncle Paul gave it to me: a scaled-down Chicago Cubs home jersey with the Wrigley Field hundred-year patch on the sleeve. A collector's item already. Uncle Paul's gifts are always the best. When I was twelve, I was going to get the coolest suit in Chicago from him, from Ralph Lauren on Michigan Avenue. But that gets ahead of the story.

I wore the Cubs jersey to school the day after my birthday. Then I had to use the restroom. You see where this is going. But I had to. Mrs. Bird gave me a restroom pass. When I got there, I went into a stall, though I didn't have to sit down. But I like my privacy.

I was just done when a foot kicked the stall door open.

I whirled around, and Jackson Showalter and I were face-to-face. I had the restroom pass, but he didn't need one. He roamed the halls at will.

He wasn't any taller than I was. He may have been a little shorter that spring. But he was like a fireplug with fists. And he was hanging with second graders, which is never a good sign. Now we were out by the sinks. We were still little guys. We had to look up to see the mirror.

But Jackson was between me and the door and getting bigger.

"Dude," he said, "I'll need your shirt."

"My uncle Paul gave me this shirt," I said, like that would do me any good.

"Skin out of it."

"I don't have anything on underneath."

He thought about making me swap shirts with him, but he decided against it. Moons and stars were on his arms. I figured I'd be seeing stars any minute now. He reached down toward his ankle with his eyes tight on me.

He came up with a knife. Not as big as the hunting knife, but a pocketknife that was all business.

He opened it, and the overhead light bounced off the blade.

"How'd you get that past the security guard?" I said in a wobbly voice.

"In my sock," he said with quiet pride. Jackson was never going to be without a knife. Even in the future, years from now—in prison—he'll have a knife. He'll make one out of a spoon or something.

He couldn't take his eyes off my Cubs shirt, but he said, "I'll just have the patch." He pointed the knife at the Wrigley Field hundredth-anniversary patch, which was what made the shirt valuable.

I decided not to cry, but I was getting there. Jackson grabbed the shoulder of the shirt and bunched it up. Then here came the knife. "Do yourself a favor and hold still." He squinted and worked the tip of the blade under the patch. "Or you'll be bleeding like a stuck hog."

It was a Swiss Army knife. I felt the flat of the blade.

The door behind Jackson banged open. Jackson jumped. He could have cut my throat. He whipped around. The school security guard filled up the doorway. He was usually out at his post, but here he was.

The knife hit the floor. "This kid pulled a knife on me," Jackson said.

"Give me a break," the guard said.

Having the guard show up at just the right time seemed too good to be true. It was. But I didn't think about it then.

He stepped around Jackson and scooped up the knife. He had a patch on his shirt too. It read: "Andy." He must have been six-five. He'd ducked in the door.

Now the tears came. I couldn't help it.

"You're the one with the restroom pass, right?" he said. "You can cut off back to your classroom."

Jackson stood there, smaller without the knife, level with the guard's kneecap. Then Andy did something surprising. He put his big hand down for Jackson to take. And Jackson took it. His hand, the one that had held the knife, disappeared into Andy's big fist.

I was just coming out of the boys' room when guess who was coming out of the girls'? Lynette Stanley, not looking my way. A girls' restroom pass fluttered in her hand.

I didn't think too much about it. I was seven. I didn't think too much about anything. I was just glad I hadn't lost the patch off my Cubs shirt.

Behind me Andy the guard was leading Jackson by the hand down to Mrs. Dempsey's office. She's the principal. Jackson was in and out of her office through the rest of his days at Westside Elementary.

5

After school, I found Grandpa sitting on a playground swing. We walked home, picking up some litter on the way.

Mom was still at work. Grown-up couples came to see her during office hours. I thought she was a wedding planner. As soon as her last customers left, she was all over the house, then all over me.

"Honey, are you all right?" She was down in a crouch, holding me at arm's length, looking me over.

I'd changed out of my Cubs shirt to keep it fresh. "Sure, why not?"

"Why not?" Mom said. "Here's why not: Jackson Showalter pulled a knife on you at school. A knife!" Mom's eyes sizzled.

"Mom, how do you even know this?"

"Because Lynette Stanley saw you get a restroom pass, and she knew that Jackson Showalter was wandering the halls. Lynette got a restroom pass herself and went straight to the security guard."

"Andy," I said.

"Whoever," Mom said. "And he found you with the Showalter gangster holding a knife to your throat. Lynette told her mother. Her mother called me."

I stubbed a toe in the rug. "I told Lynette not to."

"Not to what?" Mom said.

"Not to save me."

"You can thank your lucky stars she did," Mom said.

Stars reminded me of Jackson's arms.

Mom couldn't let it go. "Archer, honestly, I don't want to be a pushy parent. I don't want to be Elaine Schuster. But I have half a mind to go to Mrs. Bird and tell her if she can't manage her students—*first graders*—she may be in the wrong business."

"Mom, don't. Nobody can control Jackson. Nobody, Mom."

Then my uncle Paul walked in. He drove out from the city most Friday nights for dinner. He and Dad cooked, and Uncle Paul brought pizza for me.

It was the best night of the week. Uncle Paul filled a door almost like Andy. He was six-four. He'd come from work—dark suit, medium blue dress shirt. No tie. Wing-tipped shoes. No socks. Sharper than the knife in Jackson's hand.

He was carrying a pizza box and another authentic, scaled-down Chicago Cubs home jersey with the Wrigley Field hundred-year patch.

Wait a minute. "Mom, did you tell Uncle Paul about . . . you know what?"

"I told him you were assaulted with a knife."

"Mom, why?"

"Because I tell him everything that matters to me. We have no secrets. He's my brother."

They were looking at each other over my head. Uncle Paul set down the pizza but not the shirt. "Want to go for a ride?" he asked me.

"Can I drive?"

"In about nine years." Uncle Paul fished out his keys. "But not my car."

I forget what he was driving—something cool, and low. It's possible that I wasn't quite big enough to ride up front beside him. But there I was, which was great. Everything was. For one thing, Uncle Paul was the kind of grown-up who never asks you how you like school.

We pulled into a driveway that turned in a circle in front of a big house, a real McMansion. Not Grandpa Magill's kind of house. We got out, and Uncle Paul reached back in the car for the Cubs jersey.

When we were up at a big double door with carriage lights, a guy as tall as Uncle Paul opened it. He squinted at us, and there was something familiar about that squint. "Wait a minute," he said. "Don't tell me. Paul Archer."

Uncle Paul put out a hand, and the guy grabbed him in a big hug. They tussled. Then Uncle Paul said, "This is my nephew, Archer Magill."

The guy reached down to shake my hand.

"Archer, this is Mr. Showalter," Uncle Paul said.

Whoa. I was ready to run.

"Come on in," Mr. Showalter said. "You just caught me. I'm here to pick up my son, Jackson. I get him weekends. Every other weekend."

A big, glittering chandelier hung over us. Who knew Jackson Showalter was rich?

"Jackson! Get down here," Mr. Showalter bellowed up the stairs. "We're going. I'm counting to three. Bring your stuff."

He turned back to us. "Kids. Right?"

We just stood there until Mr. Showalter said, "So, you went on to Northwestern?"

Uncle Paul nodded.

"Sigma Nu?"

Uncle Paul nodded again.

"And you didn't go the hedge fund route or I'd know," Mr. Showalter said.

"No, something a lot more fun," Uncle Paul said. "I do public relations. Wrigley Field's a client."

"No way," Mr. Showalter said. "And still single?"

"Still single," Uncle Paul said.

"You were always the playboy." Mr. Showalter gave Uncle Paul a little biff on the arm.

And here came Jackson Showalter down the curving stairs with a backpack and a sleeping bag. I was kind of lurking behind Uncle Paul. Jackson saw me and stopped.

Mr. Showalter said, "Do these boys—"

"Archer and Jackson are in the same first-grade class." Uncle Paul's hand just touched my shoulder.

Jackson was up there, holding on to the banister. His starry arm looked spindly.

"Then they're friends already," Mr. Showalter said.

"No, they're not," Uncle Paul said. "I doubt if your boy has any friends. That could be one of his problems."

That stopped Mr. Showalter cold. "Wait a min—"

"He's brought at least two knives to school," Uncle Paul said, "one of them bigger than he is. And today he pulled a knife on my nephew."

"That's a big lie," Jackson hollered from the stairs. "Didn't happen."

"Jackson, go back upstairs and get your mother. I want to know if she's been hearing from school about you," Mr. Showalter said. But Jackson just stood there. "I'm counting to three," Mr. Showalter said.

Uncle Paul walked over to the stairs. He held up the Cubs jersey.

"Come on down and get your shirt, Jackson," Uncle Paul said, and waited. Jackson wanted it and didn't want it. He hung there in space. Then he started down the stairs. The chandelier glared on his skinned head.

It was real quiet. Jackson reached for the shirt. Uncle Paul handed it over. "What do you say?"

"I say that kid was the one who pulled a knife on

me," Jackson said in a high, squeaky voice, not looking down at me.

"Try again," Uncle Paul said.

Finally Jackson mumbled, "Thanks."

It was time to go. Uncle Paul said to Mr. Showalter, "It wasn't the shirt he wanted, Bob. Try to figure out what he does want."

We were in the car and halfway home when I said, "Were you and Mr. Showalter friends in high school? Like best buds?"

"Not especially," Uncle Paul said. "He was an all-around jock. He played first base and outfield and pitched eight one-hitters in his senior year. He could have gone pro, but he blew out both his knees.

"Everybody had a crush on Bob Showalter," Uncle Paul said, turning into our drive. "I think *I* had a crush on him."

A what? "You mean, like a bromance?" Which was really a fifth-grade word. I must have got it off TV. Dad and I watched a lot of TV down in the garage.

"Not even," Uncle Paul said, and killed the engine.

"What's Jackson really want?" I asked.

"For starters, a full-time dad," Uncle Paul said.

"I've got a full-time dad," I said.

"Yes, you've got a good dad."

"Remember the LEGO Ferris wheel?" I asked.

It was supposed to be a scale model of the first Ferris wheel ever, from the Chicago World's Fair of 1893. It took over half of the garage, Dad's office part. He built it through a winter when I was in preschool. Uncle Paul helped. Grandpa Magill supervised the job. They sort of forgot I was there, but it was awesome. All kinds of stuff happened in the garage.

"You've got a great dad," Uncle Paul said. "You just better hope he never grows up."

"You think you'll be a dad someday?"

"I don't know," Uncle Paul said. "First things first. But yes, I'd like to be a dad."

"And another thing."

Uncle Paul waited.

"If what Jackson wanted was a dad, how come you gave him the shirt?"

"Because now that you've been in his house, he'll leave you alone."

Then we got out of the car into the long-shadowy evening just as Dad came out of the garage with Grandpa behind him:

Dad

Uncle Paul

Grandpa Magill

These were the three I wanted to be.

6

By the way, Uncle Paul was right. Jackson Showalter kept off my case after that. He was still trouble. He gave Mrs. Bird a hard time. Once he told her where she could put Flat Stanley. But he left town that summer with his mom, and some other school got him. We haven't heard the last of him, but the good thing was he was gone.

Then came second grade, and we could all tie our shoes except for a couple of stragglers. Mrs. Canova was the teacher, and she read a bunch of picture books to us. She read *And Tango Makes Three*, which is how we found out about chinstrap penguins. And *Daddy's Roommate*.

In all the summer days between the grades Dad and I tooled around town in one vintage car after another. Once a Hudson Hornet, and usually a convertible. Grandpa rode in the back with a bottle of Gatorade. We were always paint all over from restoring another car.

Or as Holly put it, "Why can't we have regular cars like normal people? Why can't we have a Lexus like Janie Clarkson's father? A car that's just one color all over. Why doesn't Dad have a real job? Janie Clarkson's father is the CEO of something."

Holly went to driver's ed the summer she was sixteen and practiced on Grandma Magill's '92 Lincoln, which cornered like a landing craft and got eleven miles to the gallon.

In Mrs. Wainwright's third grade the standardized tests kicked in. You had to fill in all the ovals up to the edges with a special pencil.

We were taking a test one time when a cell phone rang.

Cell phones? We were third graders, and it was a no-phone school. It was Natalie Schuster's phone.

The special pencils rolled out of our hands. Anything to break up the day. Mrs. Wainwright pounded down an aisle.

By now, Natalie was taking the call. Mrs. Wainwright's face went a funny color. She put out her hand for the phone. Natalie shook her head. "It's my mother," she said. "Besides, I'm done with the test. There was nothing to it."

I forget how this scene ended, except Natalie kept her phone. As she said, her mother needed to know everything going on at school in real time.

Then it's fourth grade, with Ms. Penfield. A lot of it went over my head, including an Introduction to Fractions. Though we really got into fractions the next year.

Ms. Penfield resigned that June, but not because of us. She said standardized testing kept us from learning anything to be tested on. Her blood pressure was going through the ceiling, she said. We looked at the ceiling, and when we looked back, it seemed like she was gone.

In fourth you could walk yourself to school, so that was good and grown-up. I remembered the olden times, holding Grandpa Magill's hand all the way to school, and picking up litter.

* ❈ *

Then we had a bad night just before the start of fifth grade, a hot summer night. Some sound crept into my sleeping head, a scratching.

Now I was awake. The shadows of the backyard trees moved on the ceiling. Then that rasping sound again, on screen wire. No air-conditioning up here.

I didn't want to look. When I looked, a face in the window was looking back. Boy, that'll wake you up. Burning eyes. It was Cleo, Grandpa's cat.

But how? What combination of tree limbs and drain pipe and kitchen roof got her all the way up here? She'd never been up here, and she was no friend of mine. She didn't like kids. She didn't like anybody but Grandpa.

A claw came up again to scrape the screen. When I sat up, she knew. Still, she stayed hunkered on the windowsill, flat against the screen. Her ears pointed at the night. I switched on my lamp, and her eyes flashed yellow, and then she was gone. Like a flying squirrel, into the dark.

I sat there, groggy, not wearing much, until I realized Cleo must have come about Grandpa. That had to be it.

I threw on some clothes and detoured around

Mom and Dad's room. They'd tell me I'd had a dream.

When I started down the stairs, someone was coming up, not making a sound. Ghostly. Ghastly. Holly.

We were a step apart before she saw me. She wanted to scream, but whispered instead. "You don't see me."

"I sort of do," I said. We were *this close* to each other. Her hair smelled funny, like autumn leaves. Some dampness was coming off her like she and Janie Clarkson had snuck into the swim club pool again because one of the lifeguards—

"Why are you even awake?" she whispered. "You're never awake."

"I think something's wrong with Grandpa. I'm going over there. Tell Mom and Dad."

Holly was wearing cutoffs and a soggy tank top. "I'll have to put on my pajamas first. I haven't been out. I've been upstairs asleep for hours."

Then I was gone.

I could have circled around the block on the sidewalk, but I knew the back way by heart.

Grandpa was by the swing where Dad could watch him all day from the garage. He'd fallen on the ground, in his seersucker suit and shirt and tie. His straw hat had rolled away. He'd been waiting for the day to get going, to walk me to school. Except it was still summer, and I'd been walking myself to school for a year.

I thought he was dead. It was too dark to see breathing, so I lunged at him to drag him back. I needed him back. I wasn't done with him.

He used to let me sit on his lap behind the wheel of the Lincoln. He let me think I was steering and grown-up and driving. He kept one hand on the wheel down low, and we'd go all over town. We ran a light once, so that was the end of that.

But I didn't want him to go. He and Grandma Magill were all the grandparents I had. I could barely remember my Archer ones.

He opened an eye and looked past me up to the swing. He wanted to be up there. He sighed. Then I was yelling and yelling, till the lights came on in bedroom windows all around us. Boy, did I yell.

And somewhere Cleo was watching with her paw drawn up, then turning away.

An EMS van lumbered up the alley, flashing red and blue lights. They connected Grandpa to things and took him away on a stretcher with wheels.

Grandma Magill rode in the van with him, in the track suit she slept in. Dad followed in the Lincoln.

I wanted to go too, but Mom said no. She stood in the yard, holding her bathrobe around her. "I need you here," she said. "She has her son. I need mine."

I hadn't been needed before. It made me taller. So did the shadows.

"How did you know?" Mom asked.

"Cleo," I said, and Mom just nodded.

"Is Grandpa going to die?"

"Not if your grandma Magill has anything to say about it. I think he's had a stroke, so we won't know for a while."

I went closer, and we put our arms around each other. Then Holly was with us, in her pajamas, smelling of the chlorine from the pool. We held on to one another, trying to hold on to Grandpa. I remembered how he took Dad to the first game the Cubs played under lights, as morning crept in and fell across the empty swing.

They kept Grandpa in the hospital till after school started. Cleo wasn't around either. Grandma Magill, who hated all cats, put fresh food in Cleo's bowl on their back porch every day. Squirrels ate it, and a one-eyed cat named Sigmund Freud who lived in the corner house. Chipmunks ate it. Everybody ate Cleo's food but Cleo.

Then on the day Grandpa came home, Cleo was back in the swing, curled up asleep in a sunny patch.

So everybody was home, but Grandpa had to learn to talk again. Dad printed out a big card with the alphabet on it. Grandpa could point to letters with his good hand. That kept the conversation going until Grandpa was talking again. He never could walk, though. Dad got him up and dressed every morning, and put him to bed at night. Dad was there.

So then it was fifth grade with all the same crowd plus a new kid. Our big teeth were in, and our faces were catching up. Now I was fourth tallest behind two of the Joshes and the new kid, Raymond Petrovich, who was Gifted. Except for a girl named Esther Wilhelm, who was taller than everybody and never said anything.

Fifth grade was the year we had three different teachers and a lockdown with cops. A really good year once it got going.

We started in September with Mrs. Forsyth, who

was nice and quit at Christmas to have a baby. She turned expecting a baby into a lesson plan. We did a PowerPoint on her sonograms. She taught us fractions with her trimesters. It was all about babies until Christmas.

Then, though I didn't see this coming, Lynette Stanley and Natalie Schuster became almost friendly. They never went to each other's house. Nobody ever went to Natalie's house. You could picture it, but didn't go there. Still, Lynette and Natalie sat in the swings at noon, eating their sandwiches, throwing big words at each other.

"What's that about?" I asked Lynette. "You and Natalie?"

"I don't want her for an enemy," Lynette said. "Anyway, do *you* want to have lunch with me?"

"Not really," I said. It would have been okay except for people making comments.

I ate lunch up in the bleachers of the all-purpose room with two Joshes and Raymond Petrovich. Nobody bought the school lunch. Nobody. You brought a sandwich from home. My dad made mine.

It could be anything: leftover poached salmon on weird, foreign-tasting bread. Chutney and pepper jelly, oozing out of the bread. Sometimes a side salad in a Tupperware container with lettuce in mud colors and his own homemade croutons.

I was the only kid in school with croutons. Nobody wanted to swap lunches with me. Nobody.

One noon a few of us were having lunch when a kid ran in from outside and up the bleachers to me. He may have been a third grader.

"Hey, Archer," he yelled, "your girlfriend's beating up Natalie Schuster."

Everybody swarmed down the bleachers and out the door. Natalie and Lynette were in the dirt by the swings.

This was the first girl fight of the year. And Lynette outweighed Natalie. Lynette outweighed me. Natalie was flat on her back. Lynette straddled her. There was major hair-pulling and screaming from both of them.

As a crowd formed, the screaming let up. Lynette had Natalie pinned and spoke in a low and dangerous voice. "Take back what you said. Retract it."

"I'm taking nothing back." Natalie squirmed. "It's all true. I got it straight from the adults, and get off me, you big cow. This skirt's from Nordstrom. Where's my phone? I'm taking a selfie for evidence when my mother sues the school for having you in it, you big, fat, bovine—"

Whoa. Natalie shouldn't have used the fat word. Besides, Lynette was mostly muscle, as Natalie was finding out.

While the schoolyard held its breath, Lynette climbed off Natalie and brushed herself down. Little Josh Hunnicutt was standing right there, and his eyes were the biggest thing about him. He was still the smallest kid in our grade.

No teacher came running. Mrs. Forsyth couldn't come running. She was in her third trimester.

Natalie was sprawled out and scared to budge till Lynette moved away. I got this idea she was going to stomp on Natalie. Crazy idea, but Lynette was having it too.

Her legs shook. She was itching to jump on Natalie with both sneakers and pound her into the playground.

I came up behind her. "Better let it go, Lynette."

She whipped around, hauling off to swing. But she saw me, and her arms kind of hung down. Tears were coming, which you don't see on Lynette.

"Don't," I said. "I've got a plan."

I didn't, but I took her by the hand to walk her

out of this. Let people make comments if it made them feel better. By fifth grade can't you have the friends you want?

We'd nearly made our big exit when behind us Natalie howled out, "Lynette Stanley!" Lynette spun around, and so did I because I wouldn't let go of her hand.

Instead of a backpack, Natalie carried her stuff around in a lady's leather handbag with a Gucci bar on it and a scarf tied to the handle. She'd dumped everything out on the ground. Even her eyeliner, which she put on after she got to school. Most mornings she looked like a startled raccoon. Eyeliner in fifth grade? Yes, if you're Natalie. She'd worn it in fourth.

"Where's my phone, Lynette? Did you steal it?" She was a little braver with some daylight between them, and freaking about her phone.

"Why would I steal your phone or anything you've got?" replied Lynette in her dangerous voice. "If you can't keep track of your phone, maybe you're not mature enough to have it. Maybe your mother should cancel your contract."

Natalie seethed.

"But you can search me," Lynette said. "Though

it's only fair to warn you, if you lay one finger on me, I'll break both your arms."

I dragged her away. The first bell was about to ring. "Thanks," Lynette mumbled. "You don't have a plan. When did you ever have a plan? But thanks. I didn't leave any marks on her. I know better. But I *wanted* to stomp her."

"Oh, well," I said. "Who doesn't?"

Back there behind us, Natalie screamed, "And I still hate your hair!"

She'd pulled some of it out. The rest stood up like a big orange dandelion around Lynette's head.

"Retract?" I said to her.

"She knows the word. I suppose you want to know what the fight was about."

I was interested.

"What I tried to make her take back was true." Lynette swiped one of her eyes. "I'll put it in a note. You can read it. Can I borrow your comb?"

"You kidding me?" I said. "I don't own one." Then the first bell rang.

We had five minutes before the next bell when we were supposed to be in our seats. I hit the boys' restroom. It wasn't a problem after Jackson Showalter left except for sixth graders. When they were in there, you didn't go. You held it. But when the coast was clear, I'd drop by the restroom just to wash my hands or move my hair around a little.

It was empty except for Josh Hunnicutt, who had to stand on tiptoes at the urinal. We were both at the sinks.

He gave me a nod. Then he reached in his jeans pocket and pulled out Natalie's phone to show me.

"Whoa," I said. "Listen, Josh, that's stealing." But I was grinning.

"Not if I don't take it home," he said.

The one place Natalie had no hope of finding her phone was in the boys' restroom, right? We decided to put it up on the top of the wall of a toilet stall. Those walls don't go to the ceiling.

Josh climbed on a toilet. "Beam me up," he said, and I swung him onto my shoulders. He weighed practically nothing.

So that was that. He planted the phone up there, and we made it to class with seconds to spare.

A while later, I got Lynette's note. We were taking a quiz when this crumpled piece of paper sailed onto my desk. It said:

MY PARENTS ARE GETTING A DIVORCE—
IRRECONCILABLE DIFFERENCES.

Which was all new to me. And so was the word *irreconcilable*.

My mom hadn't said anything, even though she and Mrs. Stanley were really close. I was sorry. I thought about the Showalters, Jackson's parents, but I was sorrier for Lynette.

But we were taking a quiz, so it was more or less quiet. And from way off you could hear a tinny little song playing over and over. Natalie's phone was ringing from the boys' restroom. It was probably her mother.

Natalie herself spent the afternoon on the nurse's cot, though there wasn't a mark on her. It was going to take a couple of days before she'd confess to her mother that she'd lost her phone. But as we know, you don't slow down Natalie for long.

That would have been the day I found a grown man—in a suit—crying on our stairs when I got home. But that's another chapter.

7

I came in the front hall and the man was sitting halfway up the stairs, between me and my room. His face was in his hands, and he was sobbing.

It was sad, and surprising. He must have been one of Mom's customers. Mom herself came out of her office door and saw me down here. Then she saw the man huddled on the stairs.

"Brian, pull yourself together and go home," she called down to him. "Right now, please."

He turned and looked up at her. "What home?" His face was wet. There were tears in his stubble.

"My son is standing right there, Brian, and he doesn't need to see this," Mom said. "I don't need a parade of misery through my house."

"Right. I'm sorry." He climbed to his feet. "Sorry," he said to me, and left.

What was this about? Mom turned back to her office, and pointed me inside.

Her office desk was in the big bay window. She settled into her chair and nodded me into the sofa across from it.

"Boy," I said, "that man's really upset about his wedding plans."

Mom sagged in her chair. "Archer, do you think I'm a wedding planner?"

Yes. Of course I did.

"Archer, I'm not a wedding planner. I'm a marriage counselor. I majored in *psychology*, heaven help me."

Oh. Okay.

"People come to me when their marriages are in trouble or . . . falling apart. We talk things over very privately, very confidentially."

Right. My brain took a small leap. "Say, listen, Mom. Was that man on the stairs Lynette's dad?"

Mom blinked at me. Then she sagged some more.

"I can't answer that, Archer. And don't say anything to Lynette about—"

"Lynette knows her parents are getting a divorce. It's why she beat up Natalie Schuster."

"She couldn't know," Mom said. "They've been very careful."

But I'd kept Lynette's note. I fished it out of my pocket and handed it to Mom.

Then, speaking of misery parading through the house, the front door rattled, and Holly was home from high school.

She hit the stairs. Mom had read the note. Holly leaned in the door. "Why is a man in a Mazda crying in our driveway? And why do I even have to live in conditions like this?"

Kids know most things before their grown-ups know they know. We're older than we look. It's complicated. We're older than we act. But the whole fifth grade was in for a surprise. Lynette knew first and told me on Christmas Day.

She and her mom came to our house for dinner at noon. She was going to spend that evening with her dad, wherever he was. "Now it begins," she said. "I'm this hundred-pound Ping-Pong ball, back and forth between them. They can't get along with each other, so they cut me in two. I'm never going to do this to a child because I'm never having children. Period. End of story."

"How do you know you won't have any children?"

"Because I'm never getting married."

"How do you know that?" I said. "We're in fifth grade. How do you know all this stuff about the future?"

"Do you think *you* might want to marry me?" she asked, up in my face.

"No," I said. "Thank you."

"Then shut up," she said. This was the mood she was in as Christmas closed in on us.

Christmas Eve, it had just been the four of us, and Dad's signature chili. After that he and Mom had put on some music and rolled back the living room rug to dance.

They're not great dancers, but they don't know this. They dip and swoop and gaze away into the Christmas tree. And it always ends with a song called "I Saw Mommy Kissing Santa Claus."

"It'd be sad," said Holly, watching them from behind me, "if it wasn't so embarrassing. I'll be going away to college. Far, far away. I won't be coming home for holidays. I won't Skype."

Then the next day was a regular Christmas Day plus Lynette and her mom. Holly must have been there. I don't remember. But she wouldn't have been texting from the table because Grandma Magill was there. Dad and Uncle Paul got Grandpa Magill up the porch steps in his wheelchair. Grandma brought her famous candied parsnips.

I got some games, but it was an in-between Christmas. I wasn't too interested in clothes yet. The Ralph Lauren suit's coming, but not till next year.

The best present as usual was from Uncle Paul, earlier in December: a seat in the press box at Soldier Field for a Bears game. The Bears trounced the Dallas Cowboys 45 to 28 in wind chill at seven below. But to Bears fans it was a balmy day with a touch of spring in the air. We have to have something to believe in while the Cubs are hibernating.

On Christmas Day it was different seeing Lynette and her mother at the table. And as we know, Lynette wasn't in a great mood. Also, she was antsy because she had a secret.

"Want to see my room?" I asked her.

"Whatever," she said. "Is it a mess?"

"Do you want to see it or not?"

We excused ourselves from the table as Uncle Paul was setting fire to the pudding. Not our kind of dessert.

I'd made my bed. I make it every Christmas. Lynette scanned my room, not too interested. She was wearing a Christmas sweater with fir trees on it. Her fists were on her hips. "How do you like my sweater?"

I didn't know the answer to this. "It's . . . okay?"

"It's a nightmare," Lynette said, "like the rest of this Christmas."

"Who gave it to you?" I asked.

"Santa," Lynette said. "I could wring his neck."

"Are you going to get around to telling your secret?" I said. "Because I've been thinking. If it has any-thing to do with your parents getting a—thinking about getting a divorce, maybe my mom can talk them out of it. She's a marriage counselor, you know."

"I doubt it," Lynette said. "My mom's changed her relationship status to 'single' on Facebook."

Then she slanted a look at me, so here came the big secret. "Guess who our new teacher's going to be now that Mrs. Forsyth's gone home to have her baby."

I couldn't.

"Guess who has a teaching certificate and needs a job."

Still I had nothing.

"My mom," Lynette said.

"Your mom?" I dropped down on my bed.

"Not only do I have to have a second Christmas dinner tonight with my dad at an Applebee's, but my mom's going to be my teacher. Season's greetings," Lynette said. "Happy New Year."

8

Word got out that Mrs. Stanley was going to be our teacher, starting in January.

"Two of them!" Natalie Schuster said when she heard. "Two overbearing, know-it-all, redheaded Stanleys, like one of them wasn't enough. I don't know what my mother's going to say. I should transfer out of that school. Honestly."

If only.

You'd think it was Lynette who'd want to transfer. Picture Holly if our mom started teaching marriage counseling or whatever down at the high school. It'd be nuclear winter.

And Westside wasn't a big school. We had only

one fifth-grade class. It was Mrs. Stanley or nothing. We'd had a lady who came in to teach us art and music, but they'd downsized her.

Lynette was fairly cool about it. "It's not as bad as my dad leaving, and we need the money," she said. "But Natalie's wrong as usual. My mom's not a know-it-all. She knows no math. She's in negative numbers with math. And she doesn't know where she is with geography. And history? Grammar? Not so much."

"What did she major in?"

"Good question," Lynette said. "And she knows nothing about fifth graders. Zip."

"You're a fifth grader."

"Would you call me typical?" said Lynette, up in my face.

"Not really."

"It's my vocabulary," she said. "I'm in fifth, but my vocabulary's in senior-year A.P. English and about to graduate. With honors. My vocabulary's going to be the valedictorian. But I'm only mature compared to you. You're really taking your sweet time, you know."

"Time to what?"

"Mature," Lynette explained.

On the first day back we were all present. It was flu and cold season, but we were fine: every Josh. Esther Wilhelm sitting tall. The two girls named Emma. Gifted Raymond Petrovich. Natalie with a new phone. Various other people I haven't mentioned. Russell Beale.

Mrs. Stanley didn't start from nothing. Lynette had tried to fill her in. For one thing, even though we were a no-phones-in-the-classroom school, Natalie could have hers because nobody wanted to deal with Mrs. Schuster.

But Lynette couldn't think of everything, so Mrs. Stanley made some rookie mistakes. She called us "boys and girls" instead of "people," though that was better than "children."

Luckily, Mrs. Forsyth had left some lesson plans behind. And we were more experienced than Mrs. Stanley. We knew where the worksheets were. If you wanted a worksheet on semicolons or bar graphs, see us. And we knew where all the Common Core stuff was squirreled away. We could find the special pencils for the standardized tests.

As Lynette said, Mrs. Stanley didn't know much about fifth graders. Russell Beale, for example. He dropped off to sleep a lot, and when he did, he fell out of his chair. We were used to putting him back in it. But Mrs. Stanley was a little bit surprised the first time or two it happened.

It took her till spring to learn our names, except for Lynette and me and Natalie, whose hand was never down. But after she noticed there were seven Joshes, she'd just call out "Josh," and one of them answered. They took turns. When she wanted to call on a girl, she'd say "Emma," and one or the other would answer. Once in a while Esther Wilhelm would be an Emma and answer.

We liked Mrs. Stanley. All her quizzes were multiple-choice. But she just couldn't keep up with the paperwork, and there was a ton of it. We did the attendance report every morning and wrote somebody a pass to take it to the office. But we couldn't do it all. Printouts from the principal began to build up on Mrs. Stanley's desk.

Still, by April we figured it was smooth sailing to the end of the year. And we figured wrong. Before the week was over, we were in lockdown with a helicopter overhead. It was only a short lockdown, but we were the opening slot on the evening news.

Friday afternoons are always slower. Mrs. Stanley was at the blackboard trying to explain why you can't say "between you and I," so we may have been doing grammar. The bell rang, and we were still thirteen and a half minutes from the end of school.

Mrs. Stanley turned from the blackboard with the chalk in her hand. The voice of the principal, Mrs. Velma Dempsey, came crackling over the PA. It was the same low-tech system Grandpa Magill had installed when the school was new.

"Secure classroom doors!" came Mrs. Dempsey's voice. "Children under their desks! Lockdown! Lockdown!"

But the lock on our door was missing. Raymond Petrovich and a Josh jumped up to shove Mrs. Stanley's desk toward the door.

A bunch of us rushed to help. When Lynette put her shoulder into it, the desk shot away. Papers went everywhere. We were as secure as we were going to be. But from what?

"All right, boys and—people," Mrs. Stanley called out. "Under your desks." Stretched out, Esther Wilhelm took up the floor space under two desks, and still there was more of her. Natalie was under hers with her new phone on speed dial to her mother.

Russell Beale was under his desk and already asleep.

We weren't too worried. Anything for a change. Between you and I, it was better than grammar.

Figures raced past the windows.

"Cops!" somebody said. "A SWAT team!" They clanked like they had handcuffs hanging off them. Another couple of minutes and a helicopter was overhead. It was WGN for the local news. We got network coverage later. Basically we were about to be famous, but that gets ahead of the story.

Except for the helicopter, it was quiet. We peered from under our desks. Russell Beale stirred. Mrs. Stanley was sitting up on her desk, barring the door. A yardstick from somewhere was in her hand. She looked fierce.

Mrs. Dempsey's voice crackled again out of the PA: "Disregard the previous announcement," she said. "Resume the scheduled school day."

Like that was going to happen.

We got up. An Emma was crying, but she cried at anything. She cried at morning announcements. We helped Mrs. Stanley off her desk. "Here, give me the yardstick, Mrs. Stanley," Lynette said. She always called her mother Mrs. Stanley at school. The helicopter faded away toward Chicago. We pushed the teacher's desk back in place.

The door opened, and in walked Mrs. Dempsey. Behind her came a man in uniform. A young guy in camouflage fatigues and boots with the pants tucked in. He looked like a desert warfare action figure come to life. His hair was buzz-cut, and he was built. Not too tall, but built. He looked like he'd stepped out of a movie.

"Whoa," said several guys.

"Wow," said several girls, including Lynette and in fact Esther Wilhelm, who never said anything unless she was being an Emma.

"Mrs. Stanley," said Mrs. Dempsey, "here is your student teacher."

"I'll have to get back to you, Mother," Natalie said.

A student teacher?

We'd never had one. For all we knew, they always wore uniforms. And this one spit-shined his boots.

"Did he come in the helicopter?" somebody wanted to know. Because it would have been kind of neat if he'd been air-lifted in.

Mrs. Dempsey was in Mrs. Stanley's face, though Mrs. Stanley was bigger. "The university has sent him. Mrs. Forsyth was to oversee his student teaching, but . . . here he is. He was to have his first mentoring session after school today. There has been paperwork on this. If you had kept up with it, Mrs. Stanley, you could have averted this fiasco."

Averted.

Fiasco.

Whoa. Next to me Lynette stirred.

Mrs. Dempsey was looking at the papers curled in the corners of the room. "He arrived early and, I'm sorry to say, in uniform. Will you explain why, Mr. McLeod?"

All our eyes were on him. Mrs. Stanley's too. "I'm reporting for weekend training with my Guard unit," he said. "The Illinois National Guard."

The Illinois National Guard. How cool was that? You could see where he'd hang a row of grenades on his web belt. You could be pretty sure he had night-vision goggles.

"When Mr. McLeod entered school, Andy, the security guard, was not at his post," Mrs. Dempsey said. "When Mrs. Rosemary Kittinger, the secretary at the front desk, saw a man in uniform, she jumped to the conclusion that he was armed and dangerous."

Mrs. Dempsey still seemed to be aiming all the blame at Mrs. Stanley.

Lynette didn't like that. She could be very protective of her mother until she was about twelve. "How come Andy wasn't on duty?" Lynette's voice rang in the room.

Mrs. Dempsey wasn't used to being questioned by kids. She may never have been a teacher. But Lynette has a big mouth as we know. And in fifth grade she was just about the same size as Mrs. Dempsey.

"Since the school nurse had no record of Andy's flu shot, she called him in on his lunch break. The flu season is behind us, but better safe than sorry. Unfortunately, Andy has a problem of which we were unaware. Before the nurse could administer his shot, he fainted."

Fainted! So this was why Andy was AWOL from his post. And what a great reason it was. The idea that six-foot-five, bulging-necked Andy passed out cold at the sight of a needle was awesome.

Josh Eichenberry fell to the floor, flat on his back. His eyes rolled up. His tongue lolled. He was being Andy.

"And so alone in the outer office with a uniformed man coming into school, Mrs. Kittinger alerted the police," said Mrs. Dempsey. "We have a direct and dedicated line to the station."

She was still giving Mrs. Stanley the evil eye because she hadn't kept up on her paperwork. The yardstick was in Lynette's hand. She was thinking about giving Mrs. Dempsey a good whack around back.

Mr. McLeod looked around at us. We looked back. The girls didn't even blink. Josh Eichenberry looked back from the floor.

Then Mrs. Stanley said, "I'm pleased to have you as a student teacher, Mr. McLeod." She reached past the principal to shake his hand. "We of the fifth-grade classroom at Westside are happy to have you. We regret the welcome you've received from the school."

Mrs. Dempsey's eyes snapped. Her mouth opened and shut again.

But this was Mrs. Stanley's classroom and *her* student teacher. And she wasn't Lynette's mother for nothing. She doubled down and took over.

"I'm sorry the first person you encountered in this school was hysterical and incompetent. And I'm sorry the security guard had fainted. Heaven help us if we ever really do find ourselves under siege."

"That's all right, ma'am," said Mr. McLeod. "You can always call out the National Guard."

Mrs. Dempsey was melting down. I wondered if maybe Mrs. Stanley's teaching days were numbered. Lynette was wondering something similar.

Mrs. Stanley turned to us. There was chalk dust all down her front. "Boys and people, this is Mr. McLeod, our student teacher. What do you say to him?"

Search us. We stared. Esther Wilhelm was saying, just under her breath, "Wow wow wow wow."

"You might start with 'Good afternoon and welcome,'" Mrs. Stanley said, "and end with 'Mr. McLeod.'"

"Good afternoon and welcome, Mr. McLeod," we all said.

"Good afternoon, troops," Mr. McLeod said.

Troops! That's all we called ourselves from then on. It was way better than boys and people.

"I am a new teacher," Mrs. Stanley explained to Mr. McLeod, "and so I am just getting acquainted with these students myself, except, of course, for my daughter."

Their heads both blazed in the room. But all of us except Natalie pointed to Lynette in case Mr. McLeod had missed her.

"And you will find them the usual mixed bag of fifth graders with a lot to learn," Mrs. Stanley said.

"Their last teacher left to go on maternity leave. She seemed to have used her entire pregnancy as a lesson plan, so we may dispense with sex education. They think they know it all."

Mrs. Dempsey jumped at the sound of sex education. "Now see here," she said.

But it was true. If you wanted to know where babies came from, see us. We had the sonograms.

The end-of-school bell rang. But the PA was crackling again, with a secretary's voice. "Alert to Mrs. Dempsey! Alert to Mrs. Dempsey! The front doors are secured, but an anchorwoman from the ABC affiliate has just kicked in the lower glass panel. Alert to Mrs. Dempsey!"

Mrs. Dempsey pounded for the door, but it was blocked by a blond lady in heavy makeup with a cut on her knee. She had an ear bud in one ear. A mike was clipped to her dress. A cameraman and a lighting guy barged in behind her. The room went blinding bright, and we were all on TV. We were waving already.

"Now see here," Mrs. Dempsey said.

"We're five seconds from going live," the anchorwoman said to her. "If you're the principal, I'll need a name."

But then she saw Mr. McLeod, and the bud fell out of her ear. She fumbled for it and picked up Mr. McLeod's name from the tape on his camo jacket. "Soldier, what's your rank?" she said, very breathy.

"Warrant officer, ma'am," he said.

Then we were live. "Tell our viewers, Warrant Officer McLeod, what it's like to create a panic in a public school merely by wearing the uniform of the country you serve."

Mrs. Dempsey cringed, and we went viral.

"I was just reporting for duty," Mr. McLeod said. "Student teaching. I'm working on a master's in Elementary Education."

But the anchorwoman was already on to her follow-up question. "And what's been your combat experience? Afghanistan? The Middle East, Lib—"

"My unit hasn't been deployed since I joined," he said. "This school's about as close to combat conditions as I've come. You might want to see a medic about that knee."

The bud fell out of the anchorwoman's ear again. Mr. McLeod was right about combat conditions. Somebody from Fox News was pounding on the window. Behind him parents were rioting because they couldn't get in to collect their kids. It was basically chaos.

When school finally wound down, I found Dad out by the curb. It was a chilly Cook County April, so he was in his puffy jacket. I figured he'd be out here. He and Grandpa got the news all day in the garage on a vintage AM radio.

We crossed the street between a couple of TV vans.

"Just your ordinary school day?" Dad inquired.

"Pretty routine," I said. We stepped over the snaking cables. "We did some grammar."

It was a rainy Friday night, so Uncle Paul was there. Usually we watched sports after we ate— looked in on the Surf Dogs of San Diego or something like that. But on lockdown night we had some news shows to replay, in the garage with the space heater fired up.

I remember Uncle Paul leaning against the fender of an old Pontiac Firebird Dad was detailing. Uncle Paul with his arms folded, watching Mr. McLeod and the ABC anchorwoman with the bud falling out of her ear and all of us waving in the background.

"I think Mr. McLeod works out," I said.

"Tell me about it," Uncle Paul said.

You know the rest. The headline in the Saturday *Trib* read:

CLIMATE OF FEAR PERVADES
SUBURBAN SCHOOLS

The Sunday *News* ran a half-page picture of Mr. McLeod—Warrant Officer Ed McLeod, aged 26—under the headline:

GI Joe Reports for Duty With Fifth Graders
How'd You Like *Him* for Your
Student Teacher?

So before the weekend was over, fan pages and blogs about Mr. McLeod were all over the Internet. A ton of blogs. And he had a local fan club of au pairs. I didn't know what au pairs were. Turns out they're foreign babysitters.

Anyway, by Monday morning we were going to have the most famous student teacher in the Twitter-verse and the photosphere. And the whole rest of our fifth-grade year was nowhere near normal.

9

By the end of that next school day, the online edition of the *Trib* posted a follow-up:

RESERVIST STUDENT TEACHER SMUGGLED INTO SUBURBAN SCHOOL

Warrant Officer Ed McLeod, who caused a lockdown on Friday by turning up in uniform at a suburban school, had to be smuggled into Westside Elementary to begin his student teaching today. After a weekend firestorm of media coverage, response to his movie-star looks and starched camouflage fatigues crashed numerous social media sites. Marriage proposals were posted from as far away as North Korea.

A pop-up fan club of local au pairs

blocked the school entrance with toddlers in strollers. Mothers driving children as old as sixth grade to school created gridlock across the normally quiet suburb.

Mr. McLeod arrived on the floor of a classic Pontiac Firebird, driven by an unidentified student's father who delivered the blue-eyed National Guardsman to a disused furnace room. He was briefly sighted in civilian clothes with a large dog on a short leash, between car and furnace room door.

ABSOLUTELY NO MEDIA signs were posted throughout the school grounds. The principal, Mrs. Velma Dempsey, 52, was unavailable for comment.

Local police plan to patrol the school grounds for the foreseeable future.

Kinko's printed up those ABSOLUTELY NO MEDIA signs for Mrs. Dempsey. But how was she to get Mr. McLeod into school without being mobbed, interviewed, or proposed to? She dumped the problem on Mrs. Stanley, who called Mom Sunday night. Dad thought of the Firebird. It was a car too noticeable to be noticed, and Mr. McLeod would fit on the floor up front. Grandma Magill remembered that Grandpa had kept the keys to every building he'd ever built.

So we were all in on it. I was the unidentified student in the back of the car, next to the dog.

We'd picked up Mr. McLeod in the lot outside his gym, where he'd parked his old beat-up Kia, not the Hummer I'd hoped for. Then Dad tooled us across town. Mr. McLeod was under the dashboard. From down there he introduced me to the dog, who wanted to shake my hand. He was a Belgian Malinois named Argus.

He crowded me on the backseat and looked like he could eat your head if it was dinner time. Cops waved Dad into the parking lot at school. Then Mr. McLeod and Argus and I made a run for the furnace room door. I had the key and led them to the classroom. Lynette had come early with her mom.

"Look, no socks," she said, pointing out Mr. McLeod's ankles. He was in a dark blue blazer this morning, button-down blue shirt, maroon tie, wing-tip shoes. It would be a long time before any of us saw him in uniform again. But that gets ahead of the story.

"That's a new pantsuit on Mrs. Stanley," Lynette remarked. "And she bought all the blusher at Walgreen's. She cleared their shelves. She thought she looked too washed out on TV."

Mrs. Stanley was showing Mr. McLeod the roll book or something. Argus was stretched out in the paperwork on the floor, monitoring the room. It was the calm before the storm.

Lynette leaned over. "What's the dog about?"

"Search me," I said. "It's just his dog, I guess. It got in the car with him."

Lynette's eyes rolled. "It's not just his dog. Look at the collar on it. It's some kind of official dog, a professional. Maybe it can sniff out narcotics or dead bodies. Maybe it's trained to attack immature students who never notice anything."

"Who?" I said. "Russell Beale?"

Lynette sighed, and the room exploded with everybody else: seeing Mr. McLeod, spotting the dog, milling around. They'd fought their way through the au pairs, and they were all keyed up and unready to learn.

All the guys wanted to fist-bump Mr. McLeod. Josh Hunnicutt's fist was above his head. A couple of girls cried at the sight of him—not the usual criers. Needless to say, nobody was absent. We were hoping there'd be more helicopters. Raymond Petrovich wrote himself a pass to walk the attendance form down to the office. We never did get computerized attendance records at that school.

Raymond dodged past Mrs. Dempsey, who loomed into the room with her phone out. An unauthorized dog had been reported. Also, unauthorized people were outside our windows.

One was a big blond woman with a baby, holding up a sign that read:

HI, ED!

AU WHAT A PAIR WE'D MAKE!

"A dog, Mr. McLeod?" Mrs. Dempsey said in her voice of doom.

"Yes, ma'am, his name's Argus."

Argus arose. He was one beautiful dog, with that long muzzle and pointed ears and a brown coat with a star of white fur on his chest.

Everybody said, "Awww."

Coming to attention, Argus put up a big paw and expected Mrs. Dempsey to shake it.

"Cool," we all breathed. Mrs. Dempsey froze. But

she had to shake the paw. Argus was waiting. Just as she did, a camera flashed from somewhere.

Mrs. Stanley smiled slightly from her desk.

"Argus is a military working dog. He's the breed guarding the White House," Mr. McLeod told us, teaching already. "And the same breed the Navy SEALs used to get Osama bin Laden."

"Whoa," we said. Josh Hunnicutt was standing on his desk so he could see. Russell Beale was wide-awake.

"Argus was a scout up on the front lines," Mr. McLeod said. "He wore a tactical vest with cameras and durable microphones to relay information back to the base."

"Whoa," we said again, and "wow."

"There was a time when army dogs were put to sleep after they'd served their hitches," Mr. McLeod told us.

"NOOO!" we roared.

"But now through a Department of Defense adoption program, they're re-assigned to civilian law enforcement. Argus was a soldier. Now he's going to be a cop somewhere. My Guard unit is han-dling him while he's in transit."

Argus knew Mr. McLeod was telling us his story.

He showed us his profile. He was like a recruiting poster for dogs.

Cameras flashed again, from somewhere. We were used to them by now. It's the price of fame.

Mrs. Dempsey's mouth worked without words. What could she say about a dog who'd been safe-guarding our freedoms? Besides, Argus was practically a four-footed lesson plan. We were learning stuff this morning, and that didn't happen every day.

"Tactically brilliant," Lynette murmured. "They've got Dempsey on the run."

Mrs. Dempsey wobbled, and a camera clicked, somewhere. The phone in her hand rang. Her personal ring tone was "School days, school days, good old golden rule days." She took the call.

"NO," she barked, "absolutely *no one* is allowed in except the people replacing the glass in the front door. And where are the police who are supposed to be patrolling our perimeters? We have people with cameras in the *trees*. Never mind. I'm coming at once!" One more bleak look at Mrs. Stanley and Mrs. Dempsey was out the door.

"She called herself," Lynette remarked.

Mrs. Dempsey's picture made Tuesday's paper. She was shaking Argus's paw. Here's what the headline said:

GI JOE'S K9 ATTACK DOG WELCOMES
PRINCIPAL VELMA DEMPSEY, 52,
TO HER OWN SCHOOL

That picture practically went to the moon and back. It ended up on the website of the American Kennel Club and the *Belgian Malinois Breeders' Quarterly* and the online magazine of the Veterans of Foreign Wars. According to Lynette, it was Mrs. Stanley's screen saver.

10

Student teachers usually sit at the back, observing the real teacher for a couple of weeks. But that didn't happen.

Early in the first week Mrs. Stanley kind of bogged down on improper fractions. We knew fractions but not improper fractions. Mrs. Stanley got her numerator all balled up with her denominator.

Mr. McLeod came to the front of the room and showed us how to convert between improper fractions and mixed numbers. He drew some pie charts. So after that, he was back and forth as needed. When he turned around from the blackboard that first day, Natalie's hand was up.

"What is it, Natalie?" sighed Mrs. Stanley.

"This question is for Mr. McLeod," Natalie said.

"Is it about improper fractions?"

"Certainly not. There is nothing to them," Natalie said. "What I want to know, and I speak for the rest of the . . . troops, is do you actually intend to become a teacher, or are you going to be an actor in big-budget films? You're trending on Twitter, and the word on the *Entertainment Weekly* website is that you're scouting for an agent."

Mrs. Stanley rubbed her forehead. We were all ears. Natalie's phone was in her hand.

Mr. McLeod stroked his smooth chin.

"Being an actor would mean going out to Hollywood, right?"

We guessed so.

"Does anybody know where Hollywood is?"

Not specifically. Raymond Petrovich may have had a sketchy idea. His hand was halfway up. Some of us had been to Disneyland. Or was it Disney World?

Mr. McLeod was reaching around for something in his back pocket. "California is a couple of thousand miles from Chicago." He pulled out a Cubs cap and put it on. "And from the Cubs, so I don't think so."

Time skipped a beat. Then we were cheering. Up on our desks, doing the wave. Our eyes stung. We yelled the place down.

You could have heard us all over school. The sixth grade next door had to hear. That may have been when the trouble started. Sixth graders don't like anybody having a better time than they're having. And we had the first guy teacher in the history of the school. How annoying was that?

Mr. McLeod couldn't leave Argus at home every morning. If you didn't give the dog a job, he'd mope and get off his feed. So he was up and down the aisles like Mr. McLeod.

He herded us every day and figured out we were to be in our seats when the bell rang. He was the shepherd. We were the sheep. He was more than a dog.

Feeding him was pretty easy. After his paw-shaking picture went viral, we got over three hundred pounds of complimentary dog food. Argus had his own FedEx deliveries straight into the classroom. We were up to here with Alpo. We drew up a schedule of who'd walk him at lunch since Mr. McLeod couldn't leave the building without being mobbed, interviewed, or proposed to.

It was a really good week, except Friday was Argus's last day. He'd been re-assigned to the police force of Madison, Wisconsin.

We gave him a going-away party, of course. We broke out the dog food, and there were refreshments for the troops too. Every day that Mr. McLeod was with us, people's mothers sent pans of brownies. A ton of brownies. And the au pairs brought unusual Swedish pastries. We lived in a fog of powdered sugar.

It was a great party, as you can see on YouTube.

And the sixth graders next door no doubt heard every bark and giggle through the wall, and didn't like it. I mean—we had our own dog and baked goods, and what did they have? Long division?

Unknown hands pushed a manila envelope under the classroom door one morning the next week. It was full of dog poop. Not Argus's. So the sixth graders were really steamed.

Argus knew he was in transit and about to ship out. After his party was over and he'd licked his bowl clean, he herded us back into our seats. Then he made one last round of the rows, giving each one of us a nose bump. Russell Beale was asleep with his head on his desk, so Argus stuck his tongue into Russell's ear and moved on.

We were crying by then, and Mrs. Stanley was blowing her nose. Then Argus went for his leash and carried it in his mouth over to Mr. McLeod. Now we were sobbing.

Then just before the last bell rang, the classroom door opened, and Uncle Paul walked in. Uncle Paul out of the blue. Six foot four, in the door: hand-tailored double-breasted blazer. Brass buttons. Wingtips. No tie. Designer stubble. Unauthorized, but already in the classroom. Somewhere on him was the furnace room key that Dad had given him.

"Why, Paul," said Mrs. Stanley, who hadn't seen him since Christmas. "What on earth are you doing here?"

"I'm the backup driver," Uncle Paul said. School was officially over. We were out of our desks again, milling around—sobbing, eating brownies. It was chaos, but Uncle Paul's eyes met mine. "Your dad's taken your grandpa Magill to a doctor's appointment. Just routine."

Then here came Argus, offering a paw. Uncle Paul shook it. That gave me time to step up and make the introductions the way Grandpa had taught me.

"Uncle Paul, this is our student teacher, Mr. McLeod." Like Uncle Paul didn't already know who Mr. McLeod was. North Koreans knew. But this is how you do it.

They shook hands. Big square hands. "Ed," Mr. McLeod said.

"Paul," Uncle Paul said.

Uncle Paul and Mr. McLeod and Argus left and took me with them. Whatever Uncle Paul was driving, we weren't spotted, and Mr. McLeod didn't have to get under the dashboard.

We took him home for dinner that night, and how great was that? The most famous student teacher in the world was coming to my house—and his dog too.

As we turned into our driveway, Dad was just locking up the garage. Grandpa was there in his wheelchair, in the balmy evening. If you ask me, they looked like they hadn't been anywhere all day.

No pizza that night. I ate grown-up food. Dad served it up in his lucky apron. Mom had settled at the kitchen table between Uncle Paul and Mr. McLeod. The front door banged open and echoed through the house.

Holly.

"That'll be our daughter, Holly," Mom told Mr. McLeod. "Eleventh grade. Pretty much."

Holly seemed to be on her phone. When wasn't she? But wait. There were two voices, both whiney. Janie Clarkson?

Holly and Janie Clarkson bumbled into the kitchen. They both had their phones out. They may have been texting each other.

Argus loped over, checking them out. They froze.

Janie Clarkson spotted Mr. McLeod and couldn't believe her eyes. "I'm like wow," she said, and dropped into a chair.

It took Holly longer. If there was anybody in Illinois or the world who didn't know who Mr. McLeod was, it'd be Holly. Listen, it's possible.

Seeing Mom between him and Uncle Paul at the table, Holly closed her eyes. "Janie's staying for dinner tonight, but we don't eat whatever that is."

Dad held up a plate. "You can't get this in any restaurant."

"Please," Holly said with her eyes still closed.

* ✱ *

That was our first Friday night with Mr. McLeod. And here's how it ended. Dad thought Mr. McLeod might like to see the workshop over across the alley in Grandpa's basement. We'd told him Grandpa had been the architect of the school. Dad said I should give the tour.

Argus stayed behind in the kitchen. We'd be crossing Cleo's turf, and she didn't allow dogs. Any dogs.

When Dad headed upstairs to put Grandpa to bed, I led Uncle Paul and Mr. McLeod down to his basement.

I flipped the switch, and the whole basement lit up with hundreds of little pinpoint lights. I jumped back. There'd never been but one light down here, over Grandpa's workbench.

We three stood there on the stairs. Lights gleamed out of dozens and dozens of miniature houses. It was like being on a plane coming in over some city—Chicago, in fact.

Because over there was the LEGO Ferris wheel we'd put together when I was in preschool. Now every little car on it was lit, and the wheel was turning. Grandpa's grandpa had remembered riding it at the fair in 1893.

Grandpa had done a scale model of every house he'd ever designed and filed them all away on shelves. Now they were out and lit up. They stood in landscaped lots on Ping-Pong tables.

Over there was Westside School, except for the all-purpose room that was added later. Even the playground swings where Lynette had beaten up Natalie. Toy-car traffic crowded the curving streets.

There was more than you can imagine, including the great Chicago buildings Grandpa had studied: the Palmolive building. Navy Pier. And up a stretch of Lake Shore Drive, the centerpiece of the city: Wrigley Field, flying its flags. The ivy on the outside walls. The hand-operated scoreboard. It glowed like that first night game, 8/8/88.

A picture hung on the wall, draped in Christmas lights. Mr. McLeod studied it a long time. It was a young guy with mushroom hair and his shirt open with beads hanging down. The girl with him had flowers in her hair.

Hippies.

Love children.

Grandpa and Grandma.

All around us the lights of Grandpa's life flickered on our faces. How many hours had Dad clocked down here, putting Grandpa's life back together?

"I could have helped," I said. "I could have been down here with Dad."

"He'll need you later," Uncle Paul said.

11

Since Mr. McLeod wasn't a real teacher yet, he kept coming up with new ideas. We started every morning with some National Guard workout routines. Just what we could do next to our desks.

It woke up Russell Beale for the day, most of the day. We ran in place and did stretches, with Mr. McLeod in his shirtsleeves, being our leader.

"Really put your heart into it, Esther!" he'd call out. "Way to go, Emmas!" Mrs. Stanley exercised along with us: front squat, back squat, box squat. She was an unusual sight. According to Lynette, she lost a little over a pound and a half.

It was always something. Down in the storage room Mr. McLeod came across a stack of maps from back when there were maps in the classroom. He hung them around our walls, dusted them down, and we'd have to find places you never heard of. We tried to explain to him that we'd never need to know about these places. Kazakhstan? The Upper Peninsula of Michigan? Please. But then he'd cut out in another direction. Omaha. Omaha Beach. Selma. Wherever.

Natalie's hand was up about this, a lot. She warned him that being exposed to this much unfamiliar material could damage our self-esteems.

We racked our brains for ways to slow him down a little. "Hey, Mr. McLeod," we hollered, "when are you going to read to us?"

He looked confused. "You're kidding, right? Can't you read for yourselves?"

"Of course we can," we roared. Most of us. But we liked being read to. And we liked seeing teachers kept busy.

"Well, maybe I could read you a little from my favorite book," he said, rubbing his smooth chin. "Do you want to hear it?"

Sure. Anything.

He said it was about an army officer just back from war in Afghanistan, and looking for a guy to room with. The book was a Sherlock Holmes story by Sir Arthur Conan Doyle that just happened to be on the desk. Mr. McLeod opened it and began to read.

Who knew there were wars in Afghanistan in 1878?

Who knew where Afghanistan was?

So we were back to geography and history again before we knew it.

We liked every day to be the same, but Mr. McLeod was always looking for something new. He liked field trips. We had one a week with moms doing the driving. We seemed to have more moms than troops. We went to the arboretum twice.

There's a YouTube of us building fires to cook our lunches outdoors. We didn't have to start with flints. We could use matches, but we had to bring kindling to get a fire going. Natalie brought a commercial fireplace log with a wick, from Costco. And we hit the demo farm to watch baby pigs being born. Two Joshes threw up.

It must have been Environmental Ecology. We did a whole unit on wild plants you can eat. Dandelions, and cattails you can boil and nibble like corn on the cob. We set up a field kitchen and made soup from parboiled stinging nettles. I wouldn't want to eat it twice, but it was okay.

The field trips were great, and the moms were always ready to roll. Mrs. Eichenberry drove a showroom-fresh Mercedes, fully loaded. The only downside was that Mr. McLeod wanted us to write up reports after. This looked like homework, but Mrs. Stanley went along with it. She graded our papers. Natalie got an A-minus on one of hers, and her mother called Mrs. Dempsey about it.

Our next-to-last trip was to Wrigley Field, a VIP tour hosted by Uncle Paul with lunch in the club rooms. We didn't eat weeds that day.

It was an away day for the Cubs, so we went all over, into the dugout—everyplace. We got through the big double doors in right field to the indoor batting cages. It was like *Field of Dreams*. We jogged the bases.

We sang "Take Me Out to the Ballgame" from the box seats like it was the bottom half of the seventh. It may have been the best day of my life till then.

Uncle Paul handed Mr. McLeod a regulation bat so he could take some practice swings at home plate.

There's a ton of YouTube on Mr. McLeod taking swings and Uncle Paul watching.

The rest of us got scaled-down plastic blue-and-red Louisville Slugger souvenir bats. We battered each other senseless with them. Lynette gave Natalie a real whack around back. It was what school should be. Now we were totally used to different things on different days. Now we could do different.

You'd think they couldn't get better, but our last field trip was the best. Mr. McLeod wanted to bring the troops to Grandpa Magill's basement—that world Dad had set up.

It had really interested Mr. McLeod, who was very big on history. Our town. Chicago. Illinois. He was always amazed that we didn't know where we were.

"Point north," he'd say, and we'd point in every direction.

Dad told me I'd have to clear it with Grandma Magill first.

"Dad, you wouldn't like to clear it with Grandma for me," I said. "Would you?"

"Not really," he answered.

So one afternoon I caught up with her coming

back from a meeting of the League of Women Voters, an outfit she runs. She was aiming her Lincoln at the garage. Then she was climbing backward out of it and seeing me there.

"Archer. To what do I owe this rare visitation?"

"Hi, Grandma. I was wondering if I could bring my class to see Grandpa's basement. Like a field trip."

"*Like* a field trip?"

"A field trip."

"You want to show them your grandpa's workbench?"

"Well yes, that'd be good," I said. "And everything else."

"What else?"

"Ah," I said since she didn't know.

Her hand was on her hip. "Let's have a look down there first." We were already halfway to the basement door.

Then down we went. On the bottom step I fumbled for the light switch. Grandma was right behind me, and she wasn't crazy about surprises.

Between here and the workbench was a carpet of winking lights. Grandma's hand closed on my shoulder. She let me lead her down into Grandpa's life. Hers too. Some of the Ping-Pong tables over-lapped. You could get between others, between neighborhoods. You could take Lake Shore Drive up to Wrigley Field. Over where the lights stopped would be the nighttime lake. I hadn't looked for our own houses before.

Grandma went right to them: the pair of square houses, back to back across an alley. Aimed at the garage was a Tootsietoy Lincoln Zephyr. The wrong year, but still . . . A toothpick swing was in the yard where Grandpa always sat with Cleo. The pin-point lights sparked in the two circles of Grandma's glasses.

I walked her over to the picture framed in lights. The boy with the mushroom hair. The girl with flowers in hers. She stopped and reached out to them.

"I ironed my hair," she said. "On an ironing board. You can't imagine. And those flowers were real. Everything was."

She pointed to the boy, to Grandpa. "And that boy," she said, "I'd have followed him to the moon." She may have been crying a little bit behind her hand. I didn't mean to make her cry. I didn't know she could. But it was all right. I was there.

It was perfect attendance on the day of the last field trip.

Now that we could walk to school, we wanted to be driven everywhere else. But we walked that afternoon, just the troops and Mrs. Stanley and Mr. McLeod. A couple of die-hard au pairs with toddlers in strollers came along behind, but they fell back when we got to Grandma and Grandpa's house.

I'd already had to do an introduction in class, about Grandpa's career. Written out, of course. I'd had to use semicolons twice because Mr. McLeod really liked semicolons. I told them how Grandpa built the school and a lot of the town. How he doesn't like it when people make changes, or litter on the lawn.

There was barely room, and you had to be careful. But everybody was impressed. "Awesome," they said, and "This is as good as the Museum of Science and Industry." Little Josh Hunnicutt was totally into it. It was more his scale.

Somebody was sitting over in a shadowy corner, past the picture. Grandpa himself, though not quite full-sized anymore, sitting there, dressed in his summer suit. Only half of him worked.

I went over to him. He didn't say anything, but caught my eye with his good one, and pointed with his good hand. Dad had made a display of blueprints, rolled up and tied with ribbon. Grandpa pointed to his bad hand.

He wanted me to put a rolled-up blueprint in the hand that didn't work. When I did, it looked like he was holding it, like he was still in business. He winked at me, and I turned to the room.

"Listen, this is my grandpa, the great architect, the builder of our town." I'd told them before, but they could hear it again, and see him. "This is Mr. Addison Clark Magill, born on September 13, 1942, the day Cubs shortstop Lennie Merullo committed four errors in one inning." I told them all about him, and he smiled with half his mouth, and one eye twinkled.

Then it was time to introduce him to Mr. McLeod.

He came over, and Uncle Paul came with him. "Grandpa, this is my student teacher, Mr. McLeod. Mr. McLeod, this is my grandpa, Mr. Addison Clark Magill."

Grandpa put up his working hand. Mr. McLeod took it in both of his.

"My son has built all this to remind me of my life

and my small contribution to Chicago," Grandpa said, only a little slurry. "I believe Chicago's the finest city in the world."

"So do I, sir," Mr. McLeod said, close to Grandpa's ear because the troops were making a racket and Grandpa's hearing wasn't great.

"Are you a Chicago man?" Grandpa asked.

"No, sir," Mr. McLeod said. "I'm from Council Bluffs, Iowa."

"That where your people are?" Grandpa asked.

"No, sir. I lost my parents when I was a kid. I was fostered, and so I had many homes and none."

"Then you're welcome in this one," Grandpa said, and shifted his good eye to Uncle Paul.

12

We'd wanted to give Mr. McLeod a party on his last day. We'd given Argus a party, and we were still up to here with brownies. But the week got away. You could smell summer from here. Then it was Friday.

The first bell had rung, and we were ready for our workout. But Russell Beale was missing.

"He's not absent," Raymond Petrovich said. "I saw him coming into school."

Mrs. Stanley sent Raymond and me to check the boys' restroom. It was five minutes after the hour. You worry about sixth graders, but Raymond was about as tall as any of them. And there were two of us. Also, I was eleven. I'd had my birthday.

We ducked into the nearest boys' restroom, but it was empty. Then we thought we might as well check the one in the other wing. Andy was at his post by the front door. Mrs. Rosemary Kittinger's replacement was at the desk.

Russell was in the other restroom, watching the door when it opened. He was just standing against a sink, going nowhere. Both his hands were tied to a faucet with plastic clothesline. It was wrapped around and around and knotted tight and sealed with the faucet water. You could see how he'd tried to get loose.

But what you really noticed was the word written across his forehead in pink Day-Glo Magic Marker. Three big letters—

G A Y

"What the . . ." said Raymond.

Russell knew what they'd written on him. He could read it backward in the mirror.

Always before, he'd seemed a little younger than the rest of us. Not now. And he wasn't ready to cry yet.

We didn't talk. Raymond and I started on the

clothesline. Russell had rubbed some skin off his wrists trying to get free. We kept at it until the clothesline fell off into the sink.

I only looked at Russell in the mirror. His eyes were wet. He was checking around for the paper towels and the liquid soap. He wanted that word off him.

"I'll do it," Raymond said. Russell looked up at him, and Raymond started working over his forehead with a soapy towel. I thought it wasn't coming off. But there was pink on the paper.

The door opened behind me, and we all jumped. I hoped it was Andy. It was Mr. McLeod.

He'd come looking for us, and here we were, bunched up at the sink. Russell's face was turned to Raymond, and Raymond was scrubbing on his forehead. I was rolling up the clothesline to stick in the trash. We weren't going to say anything about this. We were going to let this go.

Mr. McLeod started to speak, but Raymond showed him the word on Russell's forehead. It was beginning to blur, but it was still there.

You could feel heat coming off Mr. McLeod. We hadn't seen him mad before. He took Russell's hands and looked at his wrists.

"Sixth graders," I said, and showed him the clothesline. I started to throw it in the trash.

But Mr. McLeod said, "No, give it to me." He stuffed it into his pocket. "They brought it from home."

"I'm not saying who they were," Russell said. "Forget that." His voice cracked and started to change right then. It was like this was the beginning of the end of being a kid for him.

I pictured Mrs. Stanley leading the workout on her own. We probably better get back to class before she tried teaching geography. You couldn't read the word on Russell now. He had some tears on his face, so Raymond handed him a dry towel without particularly looking at him.

Mr. McLeod squatted down on his heels till they were eye to eye. "Russell, will you do something for me?"

"Sure," Russell said. "Maybe."

"Will you come down to the sixth-grade class with me?"

"Whoa," said Russell.

"I'm not asking you to point out the ones who did that. I'm not going to put you on the spot. We'll bring Raymond and Archer for backup."

"Whoa," Raymond and I said.

"This is the sixth graders' last day in this school," Mr. McLeod said in a real tight voice. "Their last day. Let's not let them just walk away from this without learning anything."

Russell stood there, looking down. "You don't have to, and I'm not your real teacher," Mr. McLeod said. "But I'm going to the sixth graders anyway, and I'd like to have you with me, to see if I handle it okay. You'd be doing me a favor."

Mr. McLeod was wearing his big-toed army boots with his gray flannel pants. It wasn't his National Guard weekend as it turned out. But he only had a couple pairs of shoes: his wingtips and his army boots. He'd have had sneakers, but he was never going to be the kind of teacher who wears sneakers to school.

Something was on the floor by the toe of his boot. He picked it up. It was a pink Day-Glo Magic Marker.

"Let's do it," Russell said.

13

Then the four of us were barreling through school. Past our fifth-grade door, where the troops were clapping for jumping jacks. It was kind of a long-ago sound for some reason. We stopped outside the sixth-grade door.

I thought we might bust in. I planned to go last. But Mr. McLeod said, "Archer, go get Mrs. Dempsey. Raymond, go tell Mrs. Stanley where we are. I shouldn't be keeping you guys out of class, but this will be short and sweet."

I wasn't sure how to get Mrs. Dempsey. But in her outer office the secretary was playing video poker on her phone, so I just strolled past her. I opened a door, and Mrs. Dempsey was looking up at me from her desk.

"What is it, Archer Magill?"

"Mr. McLeod would like you to come down to the sixth grade. He can't go in there because he's not a real teacher yet. But a bunch of them tied Russell Beale to a faucet and wrote a word on his forehead."

I thought that covered it. I added "ma'am" because Mr. McLeod would. Mrs. Dempsey stared. Then she sort of erupted out of her chair and charged out the door and down the hall. I could just about keep even with her.

Leaving me and Raymond and Russell by the door, Mrs. Dempsey and Mr. McLeod walked down the hall for a little conference. He may have told her the word on Russell's forehead. When they came back, Mrs. Dempsey barged into the sixth-grade room.

The sixth graders were all over the place. The girls were in clumps of desks. The guys were up on the window ledges. Their party was to be in the afternoon. They were hanging out, waiting for that. They weren't doing anything, but you couldn't hear yourself think.

The sight of Mrs. Dempsey silenced them, but it didn't last. When Mr. McLeod walked in behind her, every girl in the room screamed. My ears rang all day. This was as close to him as they'd been. Out came the phones they weren't supposed to have. Selfie sticks—everything. The room was a zoo, a mosh pit probably.

Raymond and Russell and I came in last. They couldn't have told one fifth grader from another, except the ones who'd recognize Russell.

"Into your seats at once!" Mrs. Dempsey barked.

The guys took their time, cool and barely moving. The girls were dressed for junior high already. They were showing some skin, and you wondered about tattoos.

Their teacher, Mrs. Bickle, was older than the school. She was at her desk. A sudoku book was open in front of her.

In a doomish voice Mrs. Dempsey said, "Mrs. Bickle, kindly step next door and ask Mrs. Stanley to join us. Then will you stay with her class in her absence?"

Mrs. Bickle looked up. "I'll get right on that, Velma." She was so old, she called Mrs. Dempsey Velma. She shuffled out the door.

Then here came Mrs. Stanley, a little beaded up along the hairline from working out. She looked for Russell. When she saw him, she reached out. "Here's my lost sheep," she said.

"I wasn't lost," Russell said. "They came up behind me."

Mrs. Dempsey drew herself up. The sixth graders were waiting to find out what this was about.

"Children," she began, "as this is your last day at Westside School and Mr. McLeod's too, I'm sure you'll be glad to meet him. After all, he's put our school on the map." She looked around. No maps here.

"I know you envied the fifth graders their opportunity to learn from Mr. McLeod in Mrs. Stanley's class. Now this is an opportunity of your own to ask him anything you'd like to know."

She was setting them up for something, but they didn't suspect. We're all Gifted, of course, but they were borderline.

Mr. McLeod stepped forward. You never saw posture like that. He waited. Whimpering came from some of the girls. Finally a guy raised a casual hand. "Dude, you ever shoot anybody?"

Mrs. Dempsey sighed. Mr. McLeod said, "No, and I hope not to. I joined the National Guard because they'll pay your tuition for graduate school. I want to be a teacher. It's my goal."

The class thought that over, more or less. Phones flashed. Mrs. Dempsey said, "Speak to us of goals, Mr. McLeod. Are these children going to need goals when they get to junior high?"

"We all need goals," he said. "Here's one: Stay away from people who don't know who they are but want you to be just like them. People who'll want to label you. People who'll try to write their fears on your face."

He let them think about that; then he reached in his pants pocket and pulled out the yellow clothesline. He held it up. They watched it coil in the air. Then he pulled out the Magic Marker.

"Does anybody know who these belong to?" I don't know how he knew it, but he figured somebody was going to want to tell. And he didn't have long to wait. A gawky, hollow-chested kid at the back unfolded out of a desk. He had a flop of blond hair and was working on sideburns. He raised a big hand. All the girls dragged their eyes off Mr. McLeod. The kid pointed and said, "Jeff Spinks brought the clothesline." He pointed again. "Aidan Cooper did the lettering."

"Thanks, Perry," they muttered. "Thanks for dropping us in it." They were way down in their desks.

"And who would you be?" Mr. McLeod said.

The kid raised his eyebrows. I guess he wasn't used to people who didn't know who he was. Two girls giggled. "Perry Highsmith," he said. "Leave me out of this. I was just the lookout at the door in case anybody interrupted us. Them."

Mrs. Dempsey was turning a dangerous color. Next to me Mrs. Stanley was none too happy. Russell was on my other side, not moving.

"It was no biggie." Perry looked away through his flop of hair. "It was just like some fun on the last day. It was our *goal* to have some fun."

Mr. McLeod laid the clothesline and the marker on Mrs. Bickle's desk, like Exhibits A and B.

The girls' eyes were back and forth between Perry and Mr. McLeod. They didn't know where to look. Even scraggly sideburns are a pretty big draw in sixth grade.

"Hey, it's the last day," Perry said. "What can anybody do about it?"

In her voice of doom Mrs. Dempsey spoke. "Here's what I can do for the three of you: you Perry, you

Jeff, you Aidan. You can have your graduation party in my office while we wait for your parents to get here."

The girls murmured. Would it be a party without Perry?

Perry shrugged. Parents didn't seem to be a problem for him. He started to drop back into his seat.

"Get up," Mr. McLeod said, and waited till Perry did. "What about the word?"

"I didn't write it," Perry said. "Ask Aidan."

"What was it?" Mr. McLeod waited. Everybody did.

"It was just a word," Perry said. "It was . . . random. Ask Aidan."

Mr. McLeod waited some more.

"Gay," Perry muttered.

A whispery sound made the rounds of the room. It started out a giggle and ended with rumbling at the back.

"*Gay*'s not a random word," Mr. McLeod said. "It's an identity."

"Whatever," Perry mumbled.

"It's my identity," Mr. McLeod said.

Silence fell. You could have heard breathing, but there wasn't any.

Then one more time the girls screamed. It was ear-splitting.

With all this going on, the morning was half over before I got back to my desk. Still, Mr. McLeod was there first, holding a pointer against a map already rolled down. We were going to have an actual lesson on the last day of school. The sixth graders had already had theirs.

Lynette leaned across the aisle. "You missed Mrs. Bickle. So where were you?"

"Around," I said. "We had to get Russell out of the boys' room. Then we had to go to the sixth graders. It took a while."

"That's it?" Lynette said.

"Basically," I muttered. "Also, Mr. McLeod's gay."

Lynette's eyes practically rolled out of her head. "You really take your sweet time, don't you, Archer?"

"Time to what?"

"Mr. McLeod must really have put it out there if you picked up on it. He must have spelled it out."

It got spelled out all right, on Russell's forehead.

"Lynette, you don't know everything," I said.

But, privately, I thought she might. Anyway, it was time for map study.

By the end of the day—by noon, even—everybody knew everything. They definitely knew Mr. McLeod was gay. People in Kazakhstan knew. Bulbs flashed in the schoolyard trees.

Natalie Schuster was steamed. "Honestly, he has the scoop of the semester," she said, "and he gives it away to the sixth graders. That is so gratuitous. Men!"

A sound truck for the ABC affiliate turned into the parking lot as I headed for home that afternoon. The weekend section of the *Trib* pictured Mr. McLeod under the headline:

SORRY, LADIES

I was dragging before home was in sight. My backpack outweighed me. My ears were clanging like Big Ben.

Mom was leaning over the upstairs banister when I came in. She'd have heard all about our last day of school in real time from Mrs. Stanley. They text. I'm sure of it. But she wanted to hear the whole day from my viewpoint. She's like that.

And she was going to have to creep up on the subject because I don't tell my school day without a fight. We play this game. She'd ease in with some quirky humor. She's done it before. She'll do it again.

"Care to join me in my office?" she said. Then I was on her sofa, and she was back behind her desk. "Just a routine day?"

"Mom, you took the words right out of my mouth. We did some map study."

"Ah," said Mom. "Any place in particular?"

"Crimea? Crimea, I think."

Mom was sitting back in her chair, scanning the ceiling. Here comes the quirky humor: "Archer, honey, I think it's time we had The Talk."

"If it's about sex, Mom, Mrs. Forsyth covered it in first semester."

Mom looked sad. "Did Mrs. Forsyth tell you about the cabbage leaves?"

"Mom—"

"That's where babies come from, you know. That's where I found you, Archer, honey—under a cabbage leaf. When I brought you home, it took your dad a week to notice you. Of course when he did, he was delighted."

"Where was this cabbage leaf?" I asked.

She looked all over the ceiling, racking her brain to remember. "Washington Park," she said, "on the other side of the bandstand. That's where you came from."

"I came from the Washington Park bandstand?"

"No, honey, from under a cabbage leaf."

"Mom, Mrs. Forsyth walked us through the whole deal last fall. We have sonograms. Your water broke, and there I was. That ship has sailed."

Mom looked sad again. "Mrs. Forsyth has taken all the poetry out of the experience."

"Did you find Holly under a cabbage leaf?"

"Heavens no," Mom said. "I was in labor with her for thirty-six hours. I thought I'd die."

By the way, where was Holly? She was due to storm in any minute now. Mom's last chance to pry the school day out of me was slipping away because footsteps sounded on the stairs.

Only moments were left, which I decided to fill. "Well, thanks for sharing about the cabbage leaf. And it's not like I don't believe you. But you said one time that Grandma Magill and Mrs. Ridgley were best buds at the Salem witch trials. And, Mom, if that's true, they'd be like two hundred years old."

"I'm standing by that," Mom said.

The footsteps seemed heavier than Holly's. Mom watched the door to the hall. I watched over the back of the sofa.

Heavy treads. Muttered voices. Baritones.

Then filling the doorway was Uncle Paul, since it was getting on for Friday evening. Uncle Paul large as life: hundred-dollar haircut, manscaped stubble, a whiff of Tom Ford aftershave. And in his hand a Whole Foods sack, full of large purple growths. Eggplant. What Dad calls aubergine.

"Can you believe it?" Uncle Paul said. "Ed McLeod outs himself with no escape plan? I knew by ten o'clock, and North America knew by noon. I had to smuggle him out through the furnace room again."

I couldn't believe my ears. "You were at school, Uncle Paul? We had to clean out our cubbies today. I had to carry all my stuff home. You could have given me a lift."

I mean, why not? And I didn't see any pizza box either. Just aubergine.

"And how did you make these arrangements, Paul?" Mom inquired from the desk. She gave him her innocent look. You know how she is. "Do you have Ed McLeod's number?"

"The whole world has his number now," Uncle Paul said. "I've brought him for dinner."

"I thought you might," Mom said. "And what have you two done all afternoon? You and Ed?"

"Hung out," Uncle Paul said. "I don't know. Starbucks?"

"Starbucks," Mr. McLeod said, walking in around Uncle Paul. "Hey, Archer," he said, though we'd spent most of the day together, except for me having to walk home with ringing ears and all my stuff.

"Hey, Mr. McLeod," I said. "Crimea, right?"

"Turn left at the Black Sea," he said.

The front door banged below us. Holly. Home from high school and wherever she goes.

She'd hit the porch at her top speed and wasn't slowing for the stairs. "Mom," she screamed, getting closer and closer. "Are you sitting down? Mr. McLeod's gay!"

14

If this was a story and not real life, that Friday evening would be a good way to wind up the fifth-grade chapter. But then came three days of standardized testing to kick a hole in the next week.

We should have been out in the sun, healing from the school year. Instead, monitors worked the aisles, watching us fill in the ovals with the special pencils.

On the last day Lynette and I ate lunch together up on an all-purpose-room riser. They wouldn't let us outdoors even over lunch. Maybe they thought we'd make a run for it.

I had a Tupperware tub of what Dad calls "vichyssoise," which is cold potato soup. Don't ask. I forgot what Lynette was eating, but she didn't want any of mine.

"The school's hired Mrs. Stanley to teach fifth grade again this fall. She figures she's too famous to fire. It'd get in the papers if they didn't have her back," she said. "*I'd* call them."

"So that's great, right?"

Lynette shrugged. "At least we don't have to move."

I hadn't thought about them having to move.

"And it means Mrs. Stanley can afford to send me to camp. She and my dad are splitting the cost."

Can you picture Lynette Stanley at camp? I couldn't. Lynette around the campfire, singing along? Lynette weaving a lanyard? "What kind of camp?"

"Just a camp."

"Where is this camp?"

"Michigan." She looked away.

"The Upper Peninsula?" I said. "Because they have one, you know."

"Wherever," she said.

Now we were back at our desks. "There's no such thing as a regular camp anymore. They all have themes," said I, the big expert. I hadn't even been to day camp. Dad and I had always been too busy. We didn't do Little League either, not after T-ball. Dad said he didn't need it if I didn't.

"I bet I know what kind of camp it is," I said. "Vocabulary camp, am I right? Camp for people with over-developed vocabularies."

"Something like that," she said, very vague.

"Now that Mrs. Stanley isn't going to be your teacher anymore, are you going back to calling her Mom?"

"I think I'll stick with 'Mrs. Stanley,'" Lynette said. "I've got puberty coming up, so I need to keep my distance."

The day finally wound down. Natalie was on her feet and her phone.

"It's been a good semester for Natalie," Lynette said, handing in her last test. "She was taking pictures with her phone the whole time. Constantly. Mr. McLeod—in the classroom, at the arboretum, everywhere. She posted them, and the media picked them up. She figured out how to charge them. She made good money. She takes PayPal."

"Natalie was like a mole for the media?"

"Essentially," Lynette said. "She actually is Gifted,

the little—" The last bell rang. "And she won't be back next fall."

People milled around now, saying, "See you in sixth."

"Wait a minute," I said. "Natalie's not coming back next fall?"

Everybody was fist-bumping everybody else. Little Josh Hunnicutt was fist-bumping over his head. But Lynette was out of there. That's the end of school for you. You wait and wait. Then it's over before you're ready.

Dad was outside, set for summer: ball cap on backward, T-shirt with the cutoff sleeves. He was in Grandma and Grandpa's Lincoln. I slid in on the passenger side and buckled up.

Four or five Mr. McLeods would fit under the glove box. It was an easy car to get Grandpa in and out of, except he wasn't going anyplace now.

"Good day?" Dad inquired.

"I didn't have a day, Dad. It was testing."

"What did they test you on?"

"Dad, if I knew, I'd tell you." We rumbled off, into summer. It was only last summer, but seems longer ago.

We had a Nash Rambler that needed major restoration and paint. Ugliest car ever built, but the Nash museum in Kenosha wanted one in mint condition. We worked on that and ordered parts.

Dad and Grandma wouldn't hire anybody to be with Grandpa at night, so we were always home by evening. We carried Grandpa into the guest room, where Dad could sleep in the other bed. They didn't want him waking up to a stranger. Grandpa was like a leaf now, that thin and curling at the edges.

I woke up one night, about a month later, and the lamp was on. Mom was sitting on the edge of my bed in her robe.

She told me that Grandpa had died in his sleep, at the hospice. It's the last place you go, and Dad had been with him. I looked to see if Cleo was at the window. I looked back, and where my sheet had been was a blur. My eyes were wet.

After a minute or two, Mom said, "You need to get dressed. Your grandma has to go to the hospice. I don't want her driving herself."

Mom was in a little pool of light when I came out of my room. Holly was there, dressed, with something in her hand. She opened to show me. Car keys.

"Mom, aren't you coming?" I said. "Aren't you driving?"

"You go ahead," she said. "You need to be there. You've moved up a step, Archer."

I didn't even know what that meant. "Holly can drive," Mom said, "and you can both look after your grandma. You're Magills. Be there for each other."

"Mom, you're a Magill."

"I'm half a Magill," she said. "I'll come later when it gets light." You could smell coffee brewing in the kitchen, drifting up.

She turned away, so we were supposed to go, but Holly said, "Mom?"

And when Mom looked back, she was wiping tears away.

Holly and I went out the back way past the swing. You couldn't see where you were walking. Holly took my hand.

Then the three of us were on the Lincoln's big slab front seat. Holly behind the wheel. Me in the middle. Grandma next to me. How Holly got the Lincoln out of the garage I don't remember. I guess she found reverse.

We were heading into gray daylight. Actually,

Holly was doing okay: both hands on the wheel, both eyes on the road.

Grandma had been quiet, but now she kind of cried out. "Turn this car around! We have to go back. I've forgotten something."

I braced. There was no seat belt for the middle passenger, and I was scared Holly was going to U-turn. You don't do that in a '92 Lincoln. It's an aircraft carrier. You'd take out a front porch, and I could end up as the hood ornament.

But Holly kept going. "I didn't bring his suit," Grandma said. "I laid everything out and walked right past it. What's the matter with me?" She made fists and shook them.

"Listen, Grandma, it's okay," I said. "Dad took Grandpa's things the day after we moved him into the hospice."

"Which suit did he pick?"

"The seersucker."

"Oh, I'd have picked something darker," she said.

I didn't mention the Cubs cap. "He'll look nice in the seersucker, Grandma. He loved summer. Dad took care of it."

Then we were in the parking lot, being Magills. Holly got on Grandma's other side.

In the room Grandpa's hands were folded over the sheet. You could almost see through them. His eyes were closed, but he was squinting into the sun of an August day. So the seersucker suit was going to be all right. With the Cubs cap tucked into the inside breast pocket, over his heart. And Dad was there.

Later, when it was light, Mom came. Grandma went right over and took her hand. Then she reached for Holly. "I need my girls," Grandma said, which was a new thing we hadn't heard before.

The sun was up now, and the birds were singing. And Grandma turned to me. "Open the window, Archer," she said. "Let the birdsong in. Let Grandpa out."

So I did, and I think he breezed past me, out into the morning.

15

Grandpa was to be cremated. He left word about that. I didn't want to think about it, but he liked to keep things neat and tidy. When Dad and I went to collect his ashes, they were in this urn inside a fitted cardboard box. Dad carried it out to the Lincoln.

We were driving the Lincoln because it was all we had at the moment. The Rambler never was roadworthy.

"Should I hold him?" I meant the ashes. "Or put him on the backseat?"

I didn't know. Dad didn't know. He wore his mirror sunglasses, his shades. But I could see through them. His eyes were wet. I eased the box onto the backseat. "Remember how Grandpa liked the backseat of that Hudson Hornet convertible? He'd be back there in his Cubs cap with a bottle of Gatorade while we tooled around all over. He loved that."

Dad nodded and rubbed his stubbly chin with the back of his wrist. A thing he does. We were as quiet as we ever are, and that gave me time to think. "Do all his ashes have to go into the cemetery plot?"

We were stopped at a light. "What do you have in mind?" Dad said.

"I'm thinking, maybe you and I and Uncle Paul could take a little bit of Grandpa, maybe a handful, maybe not so much, and scatter him on Wrigley Field. He'd like being there. He always did."

The light changed. "It's probably not legal," Dad said.

"No," I said, "but we could probably get away with it."

Then we were in our driveway. Over on the swing where Cleo and Grandpa used to sit, the one-eyed cat from the corner, Sigmund Freud, was stretched out. He was making himself at home in a sunny patch, so Cleo was gone for good. Nobody ever saw her after the night Grandpa died.

Down in the garage we shook about a tablespoon-ful of ashes into an envelope. They were white and gritty. I don't know if they were Grandpa. How can you know? You can't. Dad sealed the flap with Scotch tape and handed the envelope to me.

"We—"

"No," he said. "You and your uncle Paul can take it from here. Have the time together. Anyway, I may have to raise bail money for you."

He screwed the lid back on the urn, and left a half-turn for me to do. "Are we going to tell Grandma that Grandpa's not all here?"

"*You* want to tell her?" Dad said.

"Not really," I said.

Uncle Paul picked an away day for the Cubs for our visit. The team was down in Arizona, closing a six-game road trip with another loss to the Dia-mondbacks. It was one of those days with the lake breeze rattling the ivy on the Wrigley Field walls, and summer slipping away.

We came up out of the dark of the concession area, and there it was: blue sky, green infield, dia-mond opening like a fan. One of the perfect places of this world.

It was pretty much all ours. A groundskeeping crew was working, and there were maintenance people and security. But they all knew Uncle Paul.

So nobody especially noticed when I leaned out of the stands and poured an envelope of something onto the field.

"Play ball, Grandpa," I said, and we strolled on.

Now we were up in the center-field bleachers, under the scoreboard. We had on sunscreen and our Cubs' caps. Uncle Paul had taken a rare week-day off work. Holly was up at her camp, being a counselor for its second session. Janie Clarkson went with her. The world was at peace. We were waiting for it to be noon enough for a burger down on Sheffield.

How cool was this? As cool as it gets.

"It's better without a game," Uncle Paul said, half asleep with his cap pulled down.

He was wearing deck shoes and a professionally faded golf shirt and white jeans.

"You don't wear shorts even on a day like this?"

"I'm thirty-four," he said. "That's too old to wear shorts in public."

"Tell Dad," I said.

"You tell him," he said.

I was a little groggy with the sun, but I said, "Should we be sad about Grandpa?"

"No, who wouldn't want the life he had?" Uncle Paul said. "It fit him like a glove."

That was a good thought. What else was on my mind? Oh, I know. "Dad said he might have to bail us out of jail if they caught us pouring Grandpa on the field. But I think he wanted to give us a little time to talk."

"What about, do you suppose?" Uncle Paul said.

"Search me," I said. "It could be like the talk Mom tried to have with me. The one about finding me under a cabbage leaf and being in labor with Holly for thirty-six hours."

Uncle Paul's eyes opened. "I don't believe I've heard that one. She found you where?"

"Uncle Paul, it's not worth going into. I think she wanted to talk about Mr. McLeod being gay."

"Maybe she wanted to talk about *me* being gay," Uncle Paul said.

Whoa. The sun stopped at the top of the sky.

"You knew I was gay, right?" Uncle Paul sat up, pushed his ball cap back.

"Sure," I said. "I guess. Not really. No."

"Should we have talked this over before? But your

mom and dad are so not into pigeonholing people. Were we all being so liberal, we left you out?"

I shrugged. "Lynette Stanley says you really have to spell things out for me."

"I don't mean talking down to you," Uncle Paul said. "I mean not talking past you. Not everybody in this world's so open-minded."

"Mr. McLeod told the sixth graders about people who'll write their fears on your face."

"That's good," Uncle Paul said. "You have to be ready for people like that."

My head was still kind of whirling.

Grandpa

Dad

Uncle Paul

Mr. McLeod

Those were the four I wanted to be.

"Uncle Paul, do you think I might be gay?"

"I don't know," he said. "Do you moisturize?"

"What—"

"Where do you stand on exfoliation?"

"What's ex—"

"And you didn't pick that shirt yourself, did you? Tell me you didn't."

"Uncle Paul, you're kidding me, right?"

"I'm half kidding," he said.

"One more thing then," I said. "You love men, right?"

"I love one man," Uncle Paul said.

16

Then here came sixth grade, and bring it on. We'd learned double last semester from Mrs. Stanley and Mr. McLeod. Probably triple. So what was left? And we were going to be the biggest, oldest class at Westside. Perry Highsmith and that bunch would be out of there. We'd even have a new teacher to break in. Mrs. Bickle had retired because she was older than the school.

These were my thoughts after Uncle Paul dropped me off at home that day. When I started upstairs, Mr. Stanley was coming down from Mom's office.

He wasn't crying, so I asked him how Lynette was liking camp.

He said she liked it now that she'd adjusted to it.

"I suppose she met a lot of kids with bigger ones than hers."

"*What?*" Mr. Stanley stopped dead on a step.

"Vocabularies?" I said.

"Oh," he said. Then he went on downstairs.

Mom waved me into her office. "You can be my last customer."

I settled on the sofa.

"Good day?" she asked.

"The best," I said. "We poured some of Grandpa out onto—"

Mom's hand slapped the desk. "Don't tell me that," she said. "I don't want to be responsible for knowing that."

"It's not like we're out on bail," I said.

"Nevertheless," Mom said. She might have been thinking about Grandma. "What else?"

"We had a burger and Diet Coke at a place on Sheffield. Uncle Paul didn't eat his bun, and I had all the fries. I think he's dieting, and now he's gone to work out. He may be turning into a gym rat."

"Hmmm. Possibly," Mom said. "Anything else?"

"We talked about . . . Excalibur?"

Mom pondered. "Excalibur. Isn't that a sword?"

"I think it's something you rub on your face."

"Exfoliant? You talked about exfoliant?"

"We touched on it," I said. "Uncle Paul likes to keep his skin in shape. Also, he's gay."

"Ah. Well, yes," Mom said. "We thought you'd know when you were ready to know."

"Mom, I know when somebody tells me."

Then Mom's old MacBook Air pinged, and an email came in that changed everything.

Mom put on her reading glasses. She went to a link and printed it out. Finally, she said, "Big news. You won't be going back to Westside Elementary for sixth grade."

"What? Mom, what?"

"I quote," she said. "'Due to demographic shifts in the student population, your sixth grader will transition into the former Memorial Junior High now formatted in a grades six-through-eight configuration, to be re-branded Memorial Middle School.'"

"Mom, say it in English."

"They're moving your class from elementary school to middle school," Mom said. "Monday."

I keeled over on the sofa. "Noooo."

"Honey—"

"They can't do this." I pounded a pillow. "We were going to be the oldest. Now we'll be the youngest. There'll be different teachers for different subjects. I won't be able to find them. Lockers, Mom. With combination locks."

I sat up. "Mom, I'm not ready. This isn't the body I wanted to take to middle school. Look at it. I need another year. I'm pre—what?"

"Prepubescent?" Mom offered.

"Probably. You'll have to homeschool me."

She paled. "This shouldn't come as such a shock to you," she said. "The Board of Education's been debating it all summer. It's in the paper every day."

"Mom, this is another case of everybody talking around me and not to me. I don't read the paper."

"Maybe you should."

"Maybe I would if I had my own computer with Internet ac—"

"Or you could read the one that gets thrown on our porch every morning."

"Mom, I'm not ready," I said again.

"Archer, honey, change doesn't care whether you're ready or not. Change happens anyway."

* ❈ *

Then it's the first day of school—middle school, just like that. Still August, of course. Labor Day's still down the road. They've told us sixth graders to report to the auditorium, which smells of fear. Or is it just me? I looked to see if I had the wrong shoes. I probably had the wrong shoes.

We milled around because the two homeroom teachers were up there poring over printouts. And another nightmare. It wasn't just us Westside sixth graders. It was sixth graders from Eastside Elementary and Central Elementary. A sea of strangers. I saw nobody I knew. How could that even be? A lot of friendship bracelets. A lot of headphones. A lot of hoodies. Hoodies in August?

Somebody came up to me out of the milling mob. Hoodie and shorts. Headphones and big gym shoes. Not quite my height, but his voice had changed.

"Dude, how great is it that Natalie Schuster isn't here?" he said. "She's like on the North Shore. In the New Trier district. Someplace."

"Yeah," I said. "I heard she wasn't coming back."

"Can you believe why?" this guy said.

Probably not. "Why?"

"Because her mother got married again, and they moved."

"I didn't know her mother wasn't married," I said.

"I guess we weren't supposed to. But she's married now. You know who she married?"

Search me.

"It was in the paper," this kid said. "Mr. Showalter. Remember Jackson Showalter from first grade? Didn't he pull a knife on you in the rest—"

"Right," I said. It was going to take me a while to figure this out. Natalie Schuster's stepbrother was going to be Jackson Showalter?

The guy with all the information turned away. He seemed to be working the room. He turned back. "Archer, you don't know me, do you?"

"Ah . . ."

"I'm Josh Hunnicutt."

What? "Get out of here," I said. But I looked again, and it *was* Josh Hunnicutt. The same kid, but longer.

"I grew just under a foot this summer," he said. "Eleven and three-eighths inches. Wore me out. I fainted six times. Once in the pool. They had to fish me out."

"What about the voice?"

"That's just now happening. I'm up and down with it. But it's pretty deep this morning, which is great since it's the first day of middle school."

Rub it in, I thought. "Great," I said.

"And look here." Josh pointed to his chin. "I'm about to rock some teenage acne."

"Way to go," I muttered, and he went.

Bells rang. Everybody was sitting. I looked for a seat over in the invisible section.

Nothing happened until a girl kind of slinked up to the next seat. Out of the corner of my eye she had more of a seventh-grade vibe. Was she going to sit down? She made a fist and popped me on the shoulder, hard. The pain was intense and knocked me half out of the chair.

Lynette.

"Lynette? Look at you!" I rubbed my shoulder in disbelief. There was less of her but more shape. I can't describe it. She was still eleven, but twelve was clearly on the way.

I wasn't familiar with her hair. "Lynette, what happened?"

"Camp happened." She sat down, crossed a leg. "Weight-reduction no-carbs camp."

"Wait a minute. It wasn't vocabulary camp? Because I asked your dad—"

"It was fat camp with forced marches," Lynette said.

"I thought we weren't supposed to use the fat word."

"You can use it now." Lynette looked down herself. "I had to get all new clothes. I'm going for a skirt and boots look. Is it working?"

"I guess," I said. "I mean yes. But what about your hair?"

"There was too much of it once there was less of me. I looked like a demented dandelion. After I got back to civilization, Mrs. Stanley took me for a cut and some feathering. Then we decided to tone down the color."

"You dyed your hair?"

"Rinsed," Lynette said, "with some lowlights. New school, new look, right? And how hilarious is it that Natalie's new stepbrother is Jackson Showalter— probably still two feet tall and heavily armed! You can't make this stuff up. Do you suppose the two of them were ring bearers at the wedding?"

"How did you even hear this where you were?"

"The paper. I read it online. We were really off

the grid up there in the Upper Peninsula. It was like *Hatchet*, so if I hadn't been reading the paper—"

"Right," I said. "You and Josh Hunnicutt."

Lynette pointed at the two teachers sorting us out. "You can see where that's heading," she said. "Three sixth-grade classes into two homerooms. Do the math. It won't be just our Westside class. We'll be divided up and mixed in with these other people we don't know."

I hadn't done the math.

"Poor us," Lynette said. "Poor troops. In case they split us up, meet me for lunch. Not the food court. It's what they call the cafeteria, and I'm hearing the seventh graders are going to run it as a scam. They shake you down. They charge admission, like a cover charge. But we'll only have lunch together today, because I'm going to have to find some girls to hang with. I've got some peer-grouping to do."

Now they were getting ready to divide us in half. The woman teacher was Ms. Roebuck. I never knew who the man teacher was.

"And for your information," Lynette said, "I've dropped the *ette*."

"The what?"

"The *ette*. From now on, I'm Lynn, not Lynette. I was never a Lynette anyway. It was never me, and it's not the me I want to be."

"Is Mrs. Stanley going to call you Lynn?"

"Probably not. She's too old to change, but you aren't."

Her eyebrows rose up. They were new too. Plucked or whatever. And more black than red. I squinted at her. "Who are you?" I said. "I don't know you."

"I'm Lynn," she said, and made another fist to help me remember.

17

Lockers turned out not to be a problem. Eighth graders didn't use them, and they'd won this battle long ago. Eighth graders liked the look of carrying all their stuff in a backpack from class to class all day. It worked with their casual image. Like they were just passing through. Like they'd be in high school before seventh period.

And what the eighth graders did, we all did.

But there are always myths about middle school. I can think of three, and one of them was about lockers.

MIDDLE SCHOOL MYTH #1

The administration claimed they had taken off the locker doors because people were leaving things in them, for months: smelly food, outgrown shoes, other stuff. But the story was that they'd taken off the doors when they found a human hand in a locker.

Gross, right? A human hand severed at the wrist and wearing a class ring. Sometimes an ID bracelet, but no ID. Sometimes it's a foot, with a sock.

The rest of the story was that an ancient high school had stood here before they built the middle school. Then when they were digging up the old foundation to build the new foundation, they discovered a skeleton wearing nothing but a cap that read: "Class of 1917."

In some of the tellings, the body is missing one hand. In others, both hands. Anyway, after they built the middle school, a human hand kept appearing in one locker after another. Mummified.

Annoying, and one of the main secrets of the Board of Education. You'll notice they were able to keep it out of the newspapers, which everybody but me reads.

When they got tired of burying hands in the dark of night, on school property, they took the doors off the lockers. This has solved the problem, so far. But who can say for the future? This was a story we liked better than the truth, so we sort of believed it.

And this is a total myth: that middle school teachers are smarter than elementary school teachers. Wrong, wrong, wrong. Mr. McLeod knew the most of all the teachers we'd ever had, put together. And he hadn't even graduated yet. Also, Mrs. Stanley was smarter than we'd noticed. Just to make us learn things on our own, she'd pretended not to know. Ms. Roebuck didn't have to pretend. Lynn Stanley and I ended up in her homeroom along with four Joshes, both Emmas, Esther Wilhelm, and Raymond Petrovich. And half the Eastside and Central Elementary people.

One thing about Ms. Roebuck: She was totally absentminded. She drove a Chevy Volt, and it burned a ton of gas because she'd forget to charge it up. She'd come to school smelling like an oil rig because she'd carried a can of gas down the side of the road from the Shell station, back to her Volt.

We liked her fine. She didn't yell and she never tried to tell us stories about when she went to school.

"Maybe she didn't," murmured Lynn Stanley.

I forget what she taught. It wasn't computer science. Morning attendance was computerized in a system Ms. Roebuck never got a handle on. The first day she sent out a send-all e-mail to our parents, reporting us absent. All of us.

This could have led to a parent revolt and another lockdown. An Amber Alert. Anything. But lucky for Ms. Roebuck, Raymond Petrovich was there and ready.

She got out of his way, and he sent another e-mail to our parents, countermanding the first one.

"Thank you, Josh," said Ms. Roebuck to Raymond, from the bottom of her heart. From Day One he was our permanent attendance officer. This didn't solve everything. Whenever Ms. Roebuck even walked past the computer, she'd set it off. One time parents heard that we'd been sent to the nurse. All of us. One day we all went to the counselor. "It may have something to do with her magnetic force field," Raymond said, and did what he could.

MIDDLE SCHOOL MYTH #3

If you tried to eat in the food court at noon, seventh graders would shake you down and steal your phone.

No, wait. That was no myth. That was the truth.

But Lynn Stanley had googled the school floor plan and saw that they'd drained the indoor pool for insurance reasons. She figured the room with the empty pool would be a "dank and sequestered" place that would work for our lunch.

It was dank all right. We sat on a bottom bleacher in there that first noon. She looked into my lunch. "Are those croutons? I haven't seen a crouton since June. All we ate at fat camp was kale. Bales of kale."

"What is it?"

"Like lettuce but without the personality," she said.

A chlorine smell in here reminded me of Holly on summer nights.

"You know why they drained the pool?"

"Insurance reasons?"

"Wrong," said Lynn Stanley. "The girls didn't want to get their hair wet. We may be lunching together permanently. I'm having second thoughts about peer-grouping with girls. I mean, have you seen them? And why are they all named either Sienna or Peyton? And what about the piercing on the girls from Central Elementary? What are they thinking?"

"Nothing?" I said.

"Exactly," said Lynn.

She was never going to do a lot of peer-grouping with girls. It wasn't her.

"What's in that bottle you're drinking out of?" I inquired.

"A wheatgrass smoothie." She wiped off a mustache.

"What's it taste like?"

"Like an open field," she said, "with cow pies."

Then out of nowhere she said, "I'll probably marry Raymond Petrovich. It crossed my mind when he was canceling our absences on e-mail this morning. He's a take-charge guy."

"I thought you weren't ever going to get married," I said, "end of story."

"I was in elementary school when I said that. I've moved on. And don't throw everything I say back in my face."

"Sorry."

"I'm looking for serious, not exciting. And Raymond's really smart."

"A little nerdy," I offered.

"And probably a future dot-com billionaire. We'll probably be living somewhere in the Bay Area."

"Maybe you'll marry somebody you don't meet till you're grown. Would that be so weird?"

"You can wait too long, you know, and the good ones are gone." She was looking back into my lunch. "Are you going to eat that last crouton?"

"It's yours," I said, and watched her make a meal of it.

"But what I wanted to say is, I'm sorry about your grandpa. I should have sent you a card from camp."

"It's okay," I said. "He had a good life, and it fit him like a glove. Uncle Paul and I scattered about a tablespoon of him on Wrigley Field. Then we went for a burger."

Lynn seemed to think this was fairly interesting. A lot of what I had to say didn't interest her at all.

"Did I tell you Uncle Paul's gay?" I asked.

"Did you need to?" she answered.

"Oh, right. I forgot. You know everything."

"I know *that*," Lynn said. "Where were you in second grade when Mrs. Canova read us *Daddy's Roommate*?"

"I thought it was fiction."

"Then that spring she read us *And Tango Makes Three*."

"I thought that was about penguins."

Lynn Stanley sighed.

So she wasn't all that different. New name. New shape. But basically the old Lynette, always with a plan, always knowing everything. Always thinking she could see the future.

But she couldn't.

18

Then in another week or ten days we were total middle-schoolers. We looked in the rearview mirror, and elementary school was a dot in the distance.

In homeroom we were even easing in with the other sixes, the ones from Eastside and Central. One of the Siennas—Sienna Searcy from Eastside—was a total Natalie Schuster clone.

"We're cursed," Lynn Stanley muttered. "We're doomed."

One of the guys from Central wore a T-shirt three days running that read:

ZOMBIES EAT BRAINS

SO YOU'LL BE OKAY

I wouldn't say we all bonded, but we got through homeroom together every morning.

On the Friday before Labor Day weekend the printer on Ms. Roebuck's desk spat out a message from the office. Ms. Roebuck wasn't safe around the printer either. It started printing out copies for all of us till Raymond Petrovich stepped in.

Working off the printout, Ms. Roebuck said, "Class, when you come back on Tuesday, we'll have a new member. A foreign student named Hilary Evelyn Calthorpe."

Raymond was keeping busy around her, computing the morning attendance. "What are these words, Josh?" Ms. Roebuck showed him.

"It looks like *differently abled*," Raymond said. "We could use a new ink cartridge. I'll print myself a hall pass and get one out of supplies."

So after the holiday, we'd be having a new foreign, differently abled classmate named Hilary Evelyn Calthorpe.

"Is that it? Is that all we know about this person?" Sienna Searcy barked out. "I mean, what are we supposed to do, lead her from class to class? Honestly, we already have too many people in this home-room." Sienna looked around at us. "And most of them are people you never even heard of. Seriously, what next?"

But Ms. Roebuck didn't know anything. At her elbow the printer began printing out hall passes for us all.

Then it was Saturday. Dad and I were in a rented 4x4 with a trailer hitch, pulling the vintage Nash Rambler, bound for the automobile museum in Kenosha. We were a little worried that you needed a permit to tow a vehicle on the interstate. Or as Dad put it, "Let's get an early start and hope for the best." We were wearing swim trunks under our shorts in case we found a lake to jump into.

So far so good as we pulled off for a quick break-fast. Right away the Rambler drew a crowd of car freaks with their cameras out. It never looked better: the turquoise and cream paint job, the rust-less chrome, the upholstery hand-sewn by Dad.

And when we got to Kenosha, the museum people were pretty excited. There was paperwork, and Dad is more businesslike than you'd expect. He showed me the check, and it wasn't bad for a summer's work. "Better than working the night shift at Jack in the Box," as he said.

By afternoon we were heading west on 50 toward Lake Geneva. Uncle Paul had rented a cottage up there for summer weekends, but hadn't invited us. Were we inviting ourselves?

"Are we going to Uncle Paul's place?"

"We might drop by," Dad said. "There's plenty of day left."

We came up over a rise, and there was the lake. Blue, almost black, with little white sails like sharks' teeth. Puffy clouds. Blue sky. Another perfect place, like Wrigley Field.

We crept through the town traffic. Then we were over on the Williams Bay side. We'd been up here in the winter for ice boating but now it was dense and different. We turned off the road and bumped down a track. A bunch of little cottages clustered around a pier. Two cars were pulled up on the side. One was a beat-up Kia. The other was Uncle Paul's car, a white convertible Audi A3, turbocharged. Custom cherry upholstery. Basically a dressed-up VW, but very hot, very cool.

The path between the cottages dropped down to the pier. There sat Uncle Paul in trunks and a canvas hat next to an ice chest. His feet were in the water. Another guy was on his other side, also with his feet in the water. They were sitting close, and their heads were closer.

They both looked up when they heard us. The other guy was Mr. McLeod.

I didn't see this coming.

Did you? Because I didn't.

Did they see us coming? Probably not, and Uncle Paul looked really surprised. He'd rubbed sunblock over his shoulders. He'd definitely been working out. Needless to say, so had Mr. McLeod.

"Hey, guys, sittin' on the dock of the bay?" Dad said, which may have been a code.

What were we up to?

Dad eased out of his shorts, shirt, shoes. He made a pile of them on the pier and folded his shades on top. Then he dropped into the lake in his baggy trunks.

"Hey, Uncle Paul," I said.

"Hey, Archer." He put up a big hand. He was friendly, but it was like Dad and I were crowding him a little bit.

I pointed out past the pier. "Hey, Mr. McLeod. North, right?" Since he loves directions.

"It's east, Archer. Good to see you. How's middle school?"

"We haven't learned anything yet," I told him. "We could use you back. And the brownies."

I made a pile of my clothes and jumped in the water. Dad was out there, just climbing onto the float. He has his own swimming style, but he gets there.

I don't exactly cut through the water, but I get there too. I pulled up on the float that had a little bounce to it. There's just room for two. The sun was dazzling, like diamonds on the water. We were already half dry and wouldn't be here long without sunblock. We stretched out on our stomachs.

I almost dozed, but said, "Dad, Uncle Paul said he loved somebody. You know what? I bet it's Mr. McLeod."

"You may be onto something, Archer," Dad said.

The sun was intense, but this was the last day of August. There was a little hint of something else in the air. Change.

"Dad, we didn't come up here just to jump in the lake, did we?"

"No," Dad said, "but it's great."

"And we didn't come up here just to remind Uncle Paul he'd forgotten to invite us, right?"

"No," Dad said, "but you're getting warmer."

"Dad, let's not play games. What's happening?"

"Your uncle Paul has a long history of talking himself out of relationships. He cuts and runs."

"Why does he do that?"

Dad was up on an elbow, looking back at the pier.

"I don't know," he said. "Maybe because he hadn't met Ed McLeod yet."

"Because Mr. McLeod's a keeper, right?"

"If your uncle doesn't mess up. He looks like a keeper from where I stand."

"Do you think they're alike?"

"Do you think your mom and me are alike?"

"Yikes, no way, Dad."

"I think they're a fit," he said. "But Paul has this big image—the cars, the clothes, the job, the whole package—and he kind of hides out behind it."

"So are we going to talk it over with him? Knock some sense into him?"

"No, we're guys," Dad said. "We'll talk about the Cubs, and cars."

"That'll help?"

"You work with what you've got. But we'll make sure he sees there's a place for Ed McLeod in our family. We'll keep an eye out for whatever we can do. It'll take the time it takes. It'll work or it won't work."

Now Dad was up in a crouch, and into the water. I followed. We raced, and he let me win. He'd always let me win, but now I noticed.

We sat through the afternoon, drinking canned diet tea out of the ice chest. The four of us dangled our legs off the pier: six hairy legs with big calves, plus two pale matchsticks. We talked about the Cubs and cars as the sun slid behind the trees, taking down summer.

Mr. McLeod mentioned to Dad that there were three things wrong with his Kia. Ignition and a couple of other things. Clogged fuel line. Dad said he'd have a look and put his clothes on. Mr. McLeod pulled on a T-shirt, and they went up the path to the cars.

That left me with Uncle Paul down on the pier. He doesn't know anything about what goes on under a car hood, probably because he trades them in before the first oil change. It was evening around us, but still afternoon across the lake. East. The sun was setting in their windows over there.

I looked around in my head for a good way to start. Then I thought of something. "Did Mr. McLeod ever fix you any of his stinging nettle soup?"

"His what?" Uncle Paul said.

"He can make soup out of stinging nettles."

"Not for me he can't."

"Dad says Mr. McLeod looks like a keeper to him. He was just saying that out on the float."

"A keeper?" Uncle Paul said.

I nodded. "Like you and him. Together. That'd be good, right?"

"Ah," Uncle Paul said.

"Because I think I could handle it," I said. "It'd be unusual to have your teacher in the family, but I don't think it'd be a problem for me."

"Well, that's a load off my mind," Uncle Paul said. "But there's another problem."

"What is it?" I couldn't think of one.

"You're rushing us," Uncle Paul said.

"No, we're not," I said. "It'll take the time it takes. It'll work or it won't work."

"Why does that sound exactly like your dad?"

"Search me," I said.

Long-legged bugs skimmed the surface, right where our feet were in the water. That type of bug used to freak me out when I was younger. But I'm okay with them now. It takes the time it takes.

We sat there quite a while, watching the water. And I was thinking.

"Mr. McLeod never had a dad. He told Grandpa."

"I know," Uncle Paul said.

"So if he ever wanted to be a dad—you know, down the road. Would he know how?"

"Yes," Uncle Paul said. "He'd see how your dad does it."

Then after a while Dad and Mr. McLeod came back. Dad was wiping the grease off his hands with gasoline on a rag. They trundled onto the pier.

Mr. McLeod was skinning off his shirt. He was going to take another dip in the lake. Then in a quick move he was behind Uncle Paul. He reached down and had him under the arms. He was going to hoist him up and throw him in the lake.

"No, you're not going to do that," Uncle Paul said, twisting around. "I'm bigger than you are."

"The bigger they are, the harder they fall," Mr. McLeod said.

They were both on their feet, grappling. They were basically acting a lot younger than they were, and getting closer and closer to the edge of the pier.

"No. Stop. I don't want to get my hat wet," Uncle Paul said, grunting.

"Or your hair, probably," Mr. McLeod said, also grunting.

For a second they were in the air, locked together, so they looked like a fit to me. Then a giant splat, and they were in the water, and Uncle Paul's hat was floating away. Dad was laughing, and I was there, and it was great.

We left them splashing around in the lake. We'd stretched the day as far as it would go, and we had a long drive ahead of us, Dad and I. What Mr. McLeod and Uncle Paul had ahead of them I wasn't too sure.

19

On our way home we came down through Lake Geneva city. They'd strung some colored lights down at the dock, and a band was playing. Music drifted out on the lake and grown-up couples were beginning to dance. They reminded me of Mom and Dad dancing in front of the Christmas tree.

It was dark when we hit the Illinois line. I was feeling a little older, or something. Trying to talk to Uncle Paul about him and Mr. McLeod was different for me. It was a little bit like being in middle school a year early. You're drop-kicked into new territory. I was wondering how much change you have to go through before your voice does.

I said to Dad, "I talked to Uncle Paul about how he and Mr. McLeod were getting along."

"What did you find out?" Dad said.

"You can't rush him."

"No. You can't run his race. You can just be there for him at the finish line."

"Dad, can you fix everything?"

"You mean cars?" he said. "Because I pretty much can."

"Cars are good," I said, "but I meant other stuff."

"People?"

"Yes."

"I couldn't fix your grandpa," Dad said. "I had to let him go."

So I saw Dad was still hurting about Grandpa. I didn't think about Grandpa every day now. Most days, but not every day. Dad did.

His shades were propped up on his Cubs cap. He'd be driving one-handed now, but he was setting a good example for me. It was Dad as usual, easy behind the wheel of the 4x4. But he was hurting.

"Dad, how did you meet Mom?"

"You know how. In college. I saw her in the student union one time. I had to stand up on a chair to get a better look. She was the number one most beautiful girl I'd ever seen in my life."

"So you went up to her?"

"Are you kidding?" Dad said. "I didn't know how to do that. I followed her home to the Tri Delt House."

"You stalked her?"

"We didn't have the word then," Dad said.

"Did you just trail after her until she noticed?"

"No," Dad said. "How pathetic would that be? I had a friend from home who was in Theta Chi fraternity. Jim Blassingame. We went through the yearbook and found her in the sorority picture: Marjorie Archer. Jim was the Theta Chi social chairman, so he knew the Tri Delt social chair. They set us up."

"Dad, you didn't belong to a fraternity, right?"

"No," he said. "You had to wear a tie."

Now he was braking for the Route 64 off-ramp.

"What did you say to get Mom to marry you?"

"I told her my folks owned two houses. We could live in one of them, and she'd never be homeless."

"That's it?"

"I told her she could have any guy on the campus, but she was the only girl in the world for me."

"She bought it," I said.

"You're here," he said.

Then we were home.

It was night under the trees out back. We hadn't done anything about Grandpa's swing. The only light came from high in Grandma's house, her bedroom. She wanted us to move the picture of her and Grandpa up to her living room, so we headed down to the basement. When I flipped the light, it was only the shop lighting over the workbench now. Nothing but swept concrete floor between us and the picture on the wall.

"Dad, where's Grandpa's world?"

"I boxed it back up. It was time," he said. "I guess I thought if I put his whole life down here where he could see, he'd stay a little longer."

"Maybe he did," I said.

"I hadn't thought of that," Dad said.

He was over by the workbench. Everything was in place except for a ball-peen hammer that looked like Grandpa had just put it down. Dad left it where it was and looked back at me.

"How am I going to mean as much to you as my dad meant to me?" he said.

"Dad, you do," I said. "You're there."

20

Esther Wilhelm came into homeroom Tuesday morning, tripped over her own feet, fell hard, and skinned a shin. She'd grown another couple inches over the summer and kept tripping over herself.

Then came Lynn Stanley. She was rocking a new look, showing some underwear straps under whatever else she was wearing. I didn't get it.

She dragged up the desk next to me. "Good weekend?" she inquired.

"Great. Dad and I were up at Lake—"

"So you know your uncle Paul and Mr. McLeod are an item."

I sighed. "And you know because . . ."

"Your mom, my mom—me." Lynn pointed at herself. "So do you think it's just a summer thing or serious, your uncle Paul and Mr. McLeod?"

"We're monitoring it," I said. "Dad and I. You work with what you've got, and it takes the time it takes, and it works or it doesn't work."

"I have no idea what you just said," Lynn said. "What did you bring for lunch?"

"Who, me? I never look at my lunch till I have to. Why?"

"Never mind," Lynn said. "I brought extra in case the new student didn't bring any. You know who I mean? Foreign? Differently abled? Hilary Evelyn Calthorpe?"

"Oh, right. Where is she?"

"Who?" Lynn said. "Oh. I don't know." She scanned the room. Ms. Roebuck was drifting around at the front. Raymond was taking roll. Sienna Searcy was organizing her Eastside girls. "Shut up, girls," she was saying. "I'm speaking." We were all there.

Then in the door rolled a figure in a motorized wheelchair. This stopped everything but the clock. For one thing, he was a boy.

"Now it gets interesting," Lynn remarked.

"You knew it was going to be a boy," I said.

"I googled the family, which is what Roebuck should have done."

The wheelchair made a smooth stop by the teacher's desk. He was a small, spindly kid with a cap. Not a Cubs cap. Some kind of school uniform cap. A white shirt, miniature tie, small blazer, gray flannel shorts, one gray kneesock, and a black leather shoe. The other leg stuck out straight, in a cast. You could just make out toes.

Ms. Roebuck looked down at him. "We were expecting a girl," she said.

"That's what Mother said," remarked Hilary Evelyn Calthorpe.

The room gaped. He was kind of like a doll, with bright pink cheeks and one pink knee. Ice-blue eyes that took us all in. The cap. He could have been a transfer from Hogwarts.

"Hilary and Evelyn are boys' names in England," he told us. "Evelyn with a long *e*. Why they aren't boys' names in this country I can't think, except you people get everything wrong."

We were speechless. Even Sienna Searcy. "I am differently abled for the time being," said Hilary, "because you drive on the wrong side of the road in this country. I stepped off the kerb on Michigan

Avenue in front of the consulate. That's kerb, spelled *K-E-R-B*. And I was struck from behind by an Uber car.

"If you persist in driving this way, you must simply put up signs: 'WE DRIVE ON THE WRONG SIDE OF THE ROAD. PLEASE BEAR THIS IN MIND.'"

You'll notice that we didn't all rush his wheelchair, drag him out of it, and beat him up just for looking down his English nose at us.

Ms. Roebuck was lost as always. "Well, anyway, Hilary," she said, "welcome to homeroom. What brings you to our country?"

"She should know this," Lynn muttered. "She should have googled all this."

Hilary was politely surprised she didn't know. "My mother is a diplomat. She has been made vice consul at our consulate in Chicago. She represents the United Kingdom in thirteen states."

Ms. Roebuck was blanking on this, totally. Hilary would probably have told her what a consulate is, but the bell rang. You can stretch out homeroom only so far, even in a story.

Hilary quaked. "What on earth does that bell mean? Are we under attack? Is it the Germans?"

It was first period. Except Raymond Petrovich

said to Ms. Roebuck, "He can't go to class until he's signed the anti-bullying contract. School rule."

"Oh dear," Ms. Roebuck said. "Where is one?"

"I'll print one out."

We'd all had to sign the anti-bullying contract on the first day. Absolutely no bullying allowed in this school. End of story.

"How am I to bully anyone whilst I'm in this chair?" Hilary asked. "Am I to run them down and then reverse over them?"

"Just sign here." Raymond handed him a ballpoint.

So that's how Tuesday kicked off. It wasn't a lockdown with helicopters, but it was better than nothing.

"Come on," Lynn said to me. "We'll introduce ourselves." She was up and climbing into her backpack and grabbing two lunches. We'd be late for first period, but so what? We had a lifetime supply of hall passes.

When we got up to Hilary, we just naturally bowed because he was spindly and sitting down. Lynn was a little bit shy, which was new. "Hi, I'm Lynn. This is Archer." She blushed, which was different. One of her underwear straps fell down. She worked it back with her free hand.

Hilary seemed surprised. How many middle-schoolers roll out the welcome mat for newcomers? But here we were. "Charmed," said Hilary.

"Want to have lunch with us? We have a safe place, and I've brought you yours." Lynn held up the brown bag.

"That's very kind," said Hilary, but he was sort of suspicious of the brown bag.

"I didn't know what you'd like," Lynn said. "But I knew you were English, so I brought shepherd's pie from Trader Joe's. It's thawed, but won't be hot, I'm afraid."

"Let's have a look at it," Hilary said.

Lynn lifted the lid on a Tupperware container. Hilary and I peered into it. It was a gray mass with peas.

"Oh my dear, I think not," he said to Lynn. "Let's go to the food court."

"We can't," Lynn explained. "The seventh graders would have *us* for lunch."

Hilary's eyebrows climbed up to his cap. "Really? Didn't the seventh graders have to sign that anti-bullying contract?"

"Yes, but they could also beat you to a bloody pulp," I explained. "And shake you upside down for your pocket change. They probably take PayPal. The anti-bullying contract is just to keep parents calm."

"Including the parents of bullies," Lynn said.

"Ah well, we have people for people like that." Hilary raised a small white-cuffed hand and snapped his fingers.

Everybody was heading out the door to first period. A gigantic guy was coming in. His black suit coat strained across his hulking shoulders. His hands were like catcher's mitts. It was likely he had a full set of steel teeth, except he didn't smile. Remember Andy, the security guard at Westside? This guy was bigger.

"And here is Reginald now."

Reginald?

"As long as I have to navigate a public school in a wheelchair, Lady Christobel has assigned me Reginald from the consulate security detail."

Lady Christobel?

"Lady Christobel, your mother?" Lynn said. "A lady in her own right as the daughter of the Earl of—"

"Quite." Hilary was unsurprised that Lynn knew. He also thought we ought to make it a foursome for lunch.

A foursome for lunch? We were sixth graders. What we did was more like feeding from troughs. But Hilary pointed across the room. "What about that rather striking girl who looks like the North Pole?"

It was Esther Wilhelm, fighting her way into her backpack, which tended to throw her off balance. She was about to duck out the door.

"Hey, Esther," Lynn yelled, "want to have lunch with us? Food court? We've got protection." She pointed up at Reginald. Esther stared. Then nodded. Then ducked out the door.

"She won't have much to say," Lynn told Hilary.

"Ah, but I will," he said.

We scattered for first period. Reginald too, carrying Hilary's books tied up in a strap. Behind us the printer ran off an extra class set of anti-bullying contracts.

They didn't have tables for four in the food court. "Nothing so civilized," as Hilary said. But the four of us staked out the end of a table and we were still there in the spring. Even long after the place filled up with sixth graders once they realized they didn't have to pay to get in. But that gets ahead of the story.

News of Reginald may have reached the food court before we did that first noon. But there's always somebody who doesn't get the word. And Reginald knew how to blend in, even though he was bigger than the soft drink dispenser.

A campaign was going on in the food court to wean us off sugary drinks and sodas. We were supposed to drink plain water and eat fruit or something.

"Do explain to me," said Hilary. "You aren't to eat sugar because it endangers your health, but you could be beaten to death for coming to lunch?"

That's right, we confirmed. Esther nodded.

"You really are the most extraordinary people," Hilary said. "Nothing you do makes sense."

We went for the macaroni and cheese—in fact, every day that week. Lynn did a half portion, but she drew the line at greens. Esther ate everything in sight. I don't know where she puts it. I checked the lunch Dad had packed me to see if I could salvage anything. I couldn't. We went for sugary drinks. If the seventh graders got to us before Reginald could, we were dead people anyway.

We were just tucking in when guess who loomed up? Perry Highsmith. Big seventh grader now.

Remember him? Behind him were Aidan Cooper and Jeff Spinks. Remember them?

Perry planted his hands on our table. He leaned in. "Sixth graders, am I right? Just for openers, let's see a couple of bucks all around. For the seventh-grade fund. Cash. We don't take PayPal. That's just a rumor. And I'll be back for a look at your phones after you've enjoyed dessert."

We felt Perry's hot breath. He and Hilary were nose to nose. "Oh my dear boy, those sideburns simply aren't working," Hilary said. "I'd try again in a year or two."

I thought we were dead people.

Perry flushed an ugly color. "Shut your mouth, Harry Potter, and open your wallet. Two bucks or you'll be wearing a cast on the other leg."

Hilary drew up. "I am a subject of the Queen of England," he said, "and a citizen of the United Kingdom. The sun never sets on us, and an attack upon one is an attack upon all."

"We only take U.S. money," Perry said, "and we don't make change."

Ah, but change was coming. Something like a dark cloud fell between Perry and the ceiling light.

Black-clad shoulders like giant bat wings unfurled over him. Eighth graders reached for their phones. Perry looked around, and up. And up. Reginald was there. Aidan Cooper and Jeff Spinks were walking backward to the nearest exit.

Perry made a small sound. Part of a word.

"What's he called?" Hilary asked.

"Perry Highsmith," I said.

"Listen as carefully as ever you can, Perry Highsmith," Hilary said. "Standing over you, inches away, is another Englishman. His name is Reginald, and he is my muscle. Though a man of few words, he can cause you pain that leaves no mark. Only memory."

"Ooooo," said the food court, because Hilary's voice was high but carried a mile.

"And so," said Hilary, "you are barred from this lunchroom for the rest of the year, Perry Highsmith. Until next May. Have your mother pack your lunch. Otherwise, any moneys you manage to extort in this rather badly run school will be useful for your medical expenses. There will be casts on parts of your body you didn't know you had. See him out, Reginald."

Reginald pointed Perry to the exit. Aidan and Jeff were already there.

That took care of it. A wave of applause swept the food court. Eighth graders. Seventh graders even. People who'd been conducting shakedowns twenty minutes ago were applauding. And from that day on, sixth graders thronged the place. The steam table people kept running out of food because they'd never done this much business. They couldn't keep the sugary drinks on the shelves.

In a blast from the past, Reginald even made it into the weekend edition of the *Trib*:

BRITISH BODYGUARD PROTECTS
STUDENT IN MIDDLE SCHOOL
Just How Safe Are the Leafy Suburbs
Behind Their Façade of Complacent Calm?

The *Trib* picture of Reginald was scary, so we didn't get au pairs. But by Friday people were fist-bumping our foursome on their way to the salad bar.

I forget all the things we learned just in that first week. We knew Hilary's mother was Lady Christobel in her own right. We asked him about his father.

"Daddy? Lord Horace?" he said. "He's a baron.

Lady Christobel married down a bit. When he pops his clogs, I shall be Lord Hilary Calthorpe."

"Awesome," we said. "What are you now?"

"I'm the Honourable Hilary Evelyn Calthorpe. But you never say the word. It's only for addressing a letter to me. 'The Hon. Hilary Evelyn Calthorpe,' if you write."

"Where is your daddy?" we inquired.

"The last postcard was from Acapulco. He was hang-gliding. So if you think about it, I could become Lord Hilary any moment now. A stray puff of wind. An inconvenient coral reef. Anything."

Lynn hung on Hilary's every word and brought him desserts. He could manage the wheelchair fine and wouldn't let Reginald push him. But Lynn was always hovering to help. And there wasn't any more talk out of her about marrying Raymond Petrovich and living in the Bay Area.

Hilary made a real study of us, and what he liked best were girls. He'd never been in a school with girls. "We tend not to know anything about the opposite sex until marriage," he said. "And often not then."

"You'll find the girls here a lot more mature than the boys," Lynn said.

"And yet you hide it so well," said the Hon. Hilary Calthorpe.

We thought he was weird. He thought we were weird. It was great. It was what multiculturalism ought to be.

21

After school Mom and I had a little talk in her office. The weekend *Trib* was on her desk. She tapped the JUST HOW SAFE ARE THE LEAFY SUBURBS headline.

"Why do I somehow see you mixed up in this?" she said.

"Mom, I am. I'm in a lunch foursome with Little Lord Calthorpe. He's not a lord till his daddy pops his clogs or hits a reef, but that's what everybody calls him. He's the Honourable Hilary Evelyn Calthorpe, but you never say it."

Mom watched my mouth, trying to decode what was coming out.

"You're in a lunch foursome?" Mom said. "Who are they?"

"Hilary, Esther Wilhelm, Lynn, me."

"Lynn who?"

"The former Lynette. New school, new name. She was never really a Lynette."

Mom looked at me thoughtfully. "A lunch four-some. Where is my little boy? You'll be playing bridge next."

"Mom, it could happen. Golf, even. I could tee off at any time. And we can eat in the food court since Reginald has cleared out the criminal element. It's suddenly the hottest place in town. You can't get a table.

"Mom, we're feeling a lot better with British muscle on the case."

"I wish I did," she said. "Sit down, Archer. I'd like to run a concern past you. The British Consulate people believe that the school my taxes pay for is too dangerous to attend without a . . . hit man."

"Basically," I said. "Also Hilary's in a wheelchair. He was differently abled by an Uber car because we drive on the wrong side of the road."

Again, Mom watched my mouth.

"But they'll probably keep Reginald on even after Hilary's back on his feet. Reginald has diplomatic immunity. You know what that is, Mom? He could break you in half, and they couldn't touch him."

Mom sighed. "Archer, spell this out for me as simply as you can. Why can't the school protect its own students with its own resources?"

"That's easy. Bullies have parents too, and schools don't have diplomatic immunity."

Mom searched the ceiling in her thoughtful way. "I suppose when you get to high school, Archer, you won't tell me a thing about it."

"Not a word, Mom. My secrets will be safe from you. I'll let you know when graduation is, so you can come. But not a peep out of me till then."

"All things considered," Mom said, "I think that'll be the best way." Then she went into what she really wanted to talk about. "Speaking of high school," she said, so it was going to be about Holly.

"Mom, I haven't seen Holly in days."

"Neither has the school," she said. "I got an actual call from them, not an e-mail. She's checked out of school half the time for college visits. She and Janie Clarkson seem to be hitting the open road in the

Clarksons' Lexus, making lightning raids on colleges, collecting admissions forms."

College? Holly?

"How can Holly go to college? Look at her record."

"Well, I know she failed chemistry. I thought they ought to let her repeat it."

"Mom, she blew up the lab. You had to pay for the windows. Some of her classmates still don't have their eyebrows back."

"Don't exaggerate," Mom said, and right then the front door banged downstairs. Holly was home from high school, or somewhere.

"Is Uncle Paul coming for dinner tonight?"

"I believe so," Mom said.

"Is Mr. McLeod coming with him?"

"Apparently not. I didn't like to ask."

"Mom, I hope Uncle Paul doesn't mess this up, with Mr. McLeod. You can wait too long, you know, and all the good ones are gone."

"Where did you hear that?"

"Lynn Stanley. But it'll work out, Mom. Dad and I are on the case."

"You? Your dad?" Now Mom looked really worried.

According to Hilary, the greatest talent the English have is for "administering less well-organized peoples."

And that would be us. At lunch he'd say to Esther, "Sit tall, Esther. Throw back those shoulders. Be as tall as you can be. Don't crouch. It's too late to be short."

I figured her best chance was a basketball scholarship to the U of I when the time came. But dribbling down the court in big shoes wouldn't be Hilary's idea.

"You're not jealous, are you?" I asked Lynn. "Hilary and Esther?"

"No, you buffoon," she said. "He's prepubescent, and she's seven feet tall and weighs twelve pounds. Give me a break."

Besides, his best talent was for administering the unorganized, so we all had a turn. He didn't play favorites.

But I don't care what Lynn said; she watched Hilary like a hawk. She missed one thing, though. We thought he lived in the consulate on Michigan Avenue and came out from Chicago every morning. Then somehow we learned he didn't.

"Live in the consulate?" Up went his eyebrows.

"That would be rather like living over the shop, wouldn't it?"

"Queen Elizabeth lives over the shop, doesn't she?" said Lynn. "More or less? Of course it's Buckingham Palace."

"Cousin Elizabeth? Yes, I suppose she does, really."

Cousin Elizabeth?

"You're a cousin of the Queen of England?"

"Lots of people are. She has cousins by the dozens. And we're twice married into the Harewood family, who would be her aunt Mary's people."

Lynn made a quick note on a food court napkin: *Google Harewood fam.*

"So you could end up on the throne?" we asked.

"I shouldn't think so," Hilary said. "I'm ninety-second in line."

But that didn't explain where he lived.

"Here in this town," he said. "Why would I be driven all the way out here from Chicago?"

"Because we're the center of the universe?"

"Hardly," said Hilary. "We're used to rather large houses, so Lady Christobel is renting one nearby. It belonged to a couple now divorced, I believe. The Showalters?"

"Noooo," we said. I saw it all again in my mind.

The marble floors, the chandelier gleaming on Jackson Showalter's skinned head.

"We're cursed," Lynn said. "We're doomed. We'll never be free of those people, and that includes Natalie."

We told Hilary a few things. All he'd noticed about Ms. Roebuck was that she was the worst-dressed teacher in the system.

"Maybe she's paying off a college loan," Lynn said, but it was worse than that.

What I thought was awesome about Ms. Roebuck was her allergy to the computer. She could set it off by walking by it, as we know. And the printer. And forget scanning.

This reminded Hilary of a chauffeur his family had once. "He was allergic to the steering column of the car. He once drove Lord Horace's Jag into the fountains of Trafalgar Square with all my brothers and sisters in it."

"We thought you were an only child," we said.

"I am *now*," said Hilary.

And one time Lynn said, "Archer has a gay uncle."

"Who doesn't?" said Hilary.

"It's his uncle Paul, and he's been seeing our

teacher from last year, Mr. McLeod," Lynn said. "The two best-looking guys in, like, Illinois."

"Wow, wow, wow," Esther said out of the blue, which made Hilary look.

"Archer's worried their relationship isn't going anywhere."

"I'm not worried," I said. "Don't put words in my mouth, Lynn. It is what it is and it'll work or it—"

"He's worried," Lynn said.

And now it must be October, because all around us in the food court eighth graders were taping up posters and black and orange balloons and artificial fangs. It was all about the school Halloween party, a big Memorial Middle tradition.

In elementary school, Halloween wasn't that big a deal. Cookies in shapes, a paper cup of apple juice, and make your own mask. But here it's an event: in the evening with music, dancing if you can, major costumes.

The first grown-up party of life.

Hilary may have noticed all the orange and black going up around us. Or not. He said to Esther, "Esther, you have to stop wearing that backpack. It's giving you a case of Dowager's Hump. Borrow a purse from your mother. There's no earthly need to carry all those books around. You never open them."

Then lunch was over. The bell rang, and Hilary jumped out of his skin. "I wish to heaven they'd stop ringing that thing," he said.

Reginald appeared out of nowhere, and we all scattered to fourth period.

And so went our days. They began for us all when Hilary drove his battery-powered wheelchair down the ramp out of the consular van. He seemed battery-powered himself: a mechanical mini British schoolboy in one gray sock and the uniform of a faraway school. We forgot all about how life used to be.

22

Then it's that Friday night or the next one. Uncle Paul and I are in his Audi. We're in rush hour traffic, looking for I-55.

Just as he'd walked in our house for dinner, Holly called on Janie Clarkson's phone. The Clarksons' Lexus had broken down on the shoulder of an access road. Both girls were screaming.

Mom handed the phone to Uncle Paul. "Have you called the automobile club?" he asked.

"Have we?" said Holly.

"Certainly not," Janie said. "My dad can never know we took the car, and he won't if we get it back in time tonight."

"Tell me what's wrong with it," Uncle Paul said.

"It was going," Holly said. "Then it stopped."

Could it be out of gas? Uncle Paul told them to stay in the car, lock the doors, and wait till we got there. We took a can of gas, and Dad stayed behind to cook dinner.

Now Uncle Paul and I were starting and stopping in the traffic. It was the calm before we found Janie Clarkson and Holly. It was great. I was in no hurry.

"Uncle Paul," I said. "Can I have this car in three years for my sixteenth birthday?"

"It'll be four and a half years before you're sixteen," he said, "and no."

"Shall we talk about cars and the Cubs?"

"We can if you want to."

"How's Mr. McLeod?"

"I think he's good. He has another year of course work on his degree. He has to rewrite the report on his student teaching. Apparently it reads like science fiction."

"That'd be us," I said. "What else? About Mr. McLeod?"

"The last I heard he was applying for part-time work on a road crew for the county. And this may be his weekend for the National Guard. He's got a lot going on."

"So you don't see much of him?"

"I don't see him at all, Archer. And you know something? I think it's just as well."

"How come?"

"I don't know how to explain it."

"Because I'm eleven?"

"No. It's just that he and I aren't compatible. I mean, I keep in shape. I watch what I eat. I go to the gym. But he runs seven miles before daylight and then goes to work on a road crew.

"You know what he's saving his money for?"

"A better car?"

"No, he wants to compete in a decathlon. He's saving up for the Gay Games in Paris."

Paris. I pictured Mr. McLeod sprinting under the Eiffel Tower, someplace like that. Look at him go.

"A decathlon is two days of knocking yourself out. It's javelin. It's shot put. It's pole vault and long jump. It's a half marathon. It's gymnastics—the bar, the horse. It's volleyball. Ten events. It's exhausting. You see where I'm going with this?"

"Not too well," I said. "We know he's a jock."

"He's twenty-six. I'm thirty-four. He's a kid. I'm an old man. Just naming the decathlon events put a couple years on me and gave me a shin splint."

"Do you have to compete to be compatible?" I asked.

"Don't confuse me, Archer. And stop growing up. Just be a kid."

We were seeing I-55 signs now. It was getting darker. The world was taillight red.

"It's just not workable," Uncle Paul said. "Ed's going to be starting a teaching job next fall, and where? He doesn't know. It could be anywhere. Who's not going to hire him? And sooner or later his Guard unit's going to be deployed. He's got places to go, and I'm already where I'm going. We're in different places, Archer."

"Okay," I said, "but—"

"No, wait. There's the Lexus," Uncle Paul said. "Let me finish. You need to know. Ed McLeod and I could be friends someday. Good friends maybe. But that's all. We've decided, so it's a little difficult for me to be around him. We've backed off. We've moved on."

I didn't know what to think. Should I tell Uncle

Paul that you can wait too long and then all the good ones are gone? Then I decided, no, I'd hold off till I could come up with something myself.

Now we'd eased in behind the Lexus. It was pulled up somewhere at the edge of nowhere. And yes, they were out of gas.

"Where had you been?" Uncle Paul asked them.

"Like Peoria," said Janie Clarkson.

"You were visiting Bradley University?"

"Well, that was the plan," Janie said.

"But we couldn't find it," Holly said.

We followed them home. Janie Clarkson's turn signal was on the whole time. Blinky-red-and-I'm-about-to-turn-left all the way to the off-ramp.

Then in the dark Uncle Paul said, "You're growing up, Archer."

"Not fast enough," I said. "The voice. Other stuff. Where is it?"

"It'll get here," Uncle Paul said.

"So will Christmas, but I'd like some now."

"I remember the waiting," he said.

"No, you were born six-foot-four with stubble," I said, "in those shoes."

"Oh, right," Uncle Paul said. "I forgot."

After a mile of watching the Lexus turn signal,

he said, "There's more to growing up than the voice and the other stuff."

"Mom thinks I'm making some progress," I said. "She says I'll be playing bridge pretty soon. Probably in a foursome with Little Lord Calthorpe. But then she also said she found me under a cabbage leaf, so go figure."

"You're learning to listen," Uncle Paul said. "That's more than a start."

"And the trouble with listening is you hear stuff you wish you hadn't," I said.

"That's the price you pay," said Uncle Paul.

I wasn't totally ready to move on from talking about Mr. McLeod. I was trying to work this out in my head.

"When you were twenty-six, Uncle Paul, did you date a lot of guys?"

"Yes, indeedy," he said.

"Were you, like, in love with any of them?"

"I tried to be, but no," he said. "That's why this hits me so hard now."

"Because of love?" I said. It was dark.

"Yes," he said.

"Then how can you and Mr. McLeod ever just be friends?"

"Don't confuse me, Archer."

"Okay then, just one more question, but it's easy. When did you decide to be gay, Uncle Paul?"

"Being gay isn't a decision. How you live your life is a decision."

"Oh, okay," I said. "Right."

23

The next week was all about the school Halloween party. A planning committee of seventh and eighth graders were busy as bees, or at least out of class. Tuesday in homeroom we got an incoming e-mail.

"Step away from the screen, Ms. Roebuck," Raymond Petrovich said, and read out a message from the principal's office.

Students of Memorial Middle School:
The Excitement mounts as Halloween approaches in a whirl of autumn leaves and anticipation. The Halloween party as

you know is one of the school's most trea-sured traditions, dating from our days as a junior high.

With that heritage in mind, we have hon-ored the request of the seventh and eighth graders to limit this gala evening to their two classes.

We are unanimous in our welcome of a promising class of sixth graders for the first time in the school's history. But we acknowledge the need for the seventh and eighth graders to enjoy an evening without the company of a class that is in effect still elementary-school age and not yet "party ready."

That doesn't mean the sixes won't have their own celebration of the season, and a fine one too! The sixth-grade festivities will take place on the last period of Halloween Friday, with plenty of cookies and apple juice for all, and a craft table for making their own masks. Ghosts! Goblins! And forty-five minutes of fun.

The seventh- and eighth-grade extrava-ganza, "Dracula's Dungeon," will take place in the food court. Music from 7:30, buffet refreshments from 8.

A heartfelt happy Halloween to all,

(signed)

Mr. Otto Kleinfelt, Principal

Mrs. P. T. Highsmith,

President, Parent Teacher Association

We heard this document to the bitter end, read out in Raymond's creaky tenor. We were totally steamed. Then Sienna Searcy rose out of her girls to say, "I'll be fine. I'm going to Dracula's Dungeon as an eighth grader's date. Liam Carmichael."

"Does he know?" snapped an Emma.

"They're treating us like babies," said a Central girl. Peyton somebody. "I know what: Let's all wear Pampers on Friday."

Which nobody wanted to do.

"Apple juice," people said. "Could you puke?"

Everybody agreed it was a crime and totally not fair. We said we wouldn't go to this so-called forty-five-minute party. We'd cut out of school early. We all had hall passes.

"We're going public with this," Lynn Stanley barked. "We Westsiders know plenty about the power of the media. We can go viral because this story has legs. We want some serious ink on this, and I'm seeing a headline in the *Sun-Times*: UNHAPPY HALLOWEEN FOR MEMORIAL MIDDLE 6TH GRADERS BANNED FROM ANNUAL PARTY."

This got some applause, but Hilary only looked on, cool as his usual self. His wheelchair was parked at a slant in front of Lynn and me. His naked toes twinkled at her from the end of his cast. "Try to keep calm, Lynn," he remarked.

"Why should I?" she said, very snappish.

"Because we shall get more serious ink than ever you can think."

"How will this happen, Hilary?" Her eyes narrowed. She was using a little eyeliner these days.

"Because we sixth graders will have a Halloween party that will make their Dracula's Dungeon look like detention."

Hilary shifted down and motored to the front of the room, turning on a dime. He was English, and we were a less well-organized people. He looked us over.

Ms. Roebuck bent to tie the shoelace on one of her sneakers, and the printer printed out a class set of the letter from the principal and Mrs. Highsmith.

"Our party will take place when their party takes place," Hilary announced. "But ours won't be in a cafeteria reeking of bad pizza."

"Then where?" people wondered. Not the swimming pool room. Too dank.

"At the Calthorpe residence," said Hilary.

"Ah, the old Showalter place," Lynn muttered. "Talk about a haunted house."

"Halloween is rather Scottish," Hilary explained, "but the English invented the fancy-dress party. Lady Christobel has a dozen trunks full of quite wonderful costumes, many of them historic." Hilary's glance swept over Lynn and me, then fell on Ms. Roebuck.

She was smoothing out her skirt.

"Ms. Roebuck, you're to be a chaperone if we can find a suitable escort for you," Hilary told her.

Hope chased fear across Ms. Roebuck's face. Her skirt swept a keyboard, and our parents got an e-mail about flu shots.

"Raymond?" Hilary wheeled around. "Where are you? There you are. Get out word about our party to the other sixth-grade homeroom. Lynn Stanley, be secretary and draw up a list. We will of course need quite an army of adults to chaperone us since we aren't party ready." His piping voice dripped British sarcasm.

Lynn had already whipped out a notepad. The first name on her list was

PAUL ARCHER,

who'd be a great chaperone.

Lynn stroked a cheek and added

MR. & MRS. BRIAN STANLEY,

her parents.

"We'll need them both," she said. "I always did."

She went on with the list and put down all our teachers from this year and last. Making up the list seemed to be a power surge for her.

Up at the front Hilary was saying, "We have ahead of us a busy week of planning. Don't think of trying to learn anything. Keep your minds perfect blanks in class."

"Say, listen," Sienna Searcy said from out of her group, "who is this Lady Christobel person anyway?"

"My dear, you'll never know," Hilary said to her. "You'll be at the wrong party."

The bell rang, and Hilary jumped. Reginald

loomed in. Then we were off to first period, careful
to keep our minds perfect blanks.

Lynn Stanley didn't get her UNHAPPY HALLOW-
EEN headline into the *Sun-Times*. But somebody
did, and as soon as Wednesday. Probably somebody
better organized:

PARTY OF SEASON PLANNED FOR
SNUBBED 6TH GRADERS

When a sixth grader at Memorial Middle
School came home to tell his mother that
his class had been barred from the school's
Halloween party, the idea of the event of
the social season was born.

The mother is Lady Christobel Calthorpe,
vice consul of the British Consulate. The
son is the Hon. Hilary Evelyn Calthorpe,
future Baron Calthorpe of Calthorpe Castle
in England.

The family is presently at home, unex-
pectedly, in the western suburbs. But in a
graciously granted phone interview, Lady
Christobel said, "We are English, and so

we have held quite memorable events in remoter regions than these. The Charge of the Light Brigade comes to mind. And I have behind me the resources of the British Consulate, and behind them the United Kingdom."

Her Ladyship added that while Halloween is not an essentially English holiday, "We know all there is to know about dressing up."

Given the Calthorpe glamour and grandeur (Lady Christobel is ninety-first in line for the throne) the party promises to be a hot ticket, one unlikely to be limited to sixth graders.

Otto Kleinfelt, principal of Memorial Middle School, was unavailable for comment.

24

You can get invitations engraved overnight if you're the British Consulate with the full force of the United Kingdom behind you. Ours was addressed to THE MAGILL FAMILY on paper so thick it unfolded itself. It was *this close* to a royal command.

Dad was totally stoked. You'd think the last thing he'd want to do is dress up for a party. But he worked around the clock on our costumes. Mom had to cook for the rest of the week.

I'd planned to glue straggly wood shavings down both sides of my face, top off with a floppy yellow nylon wig, and go as Perry Highsmith. But Dad had other plans.

In case you didn't recognize us at the party, we were three characters from *The Wizard of Oz*— Scarecrow (Mom), Cowardly Lion (me) (thanks, Dad), and Tin Man (Dad).

It all had to be just right. Dad drove out to Long Grove for actual straw to stuff up Mom's sleeves. Grandma Magill had been leading a quiet life since Grandpa died, but she brought out her sewing machine. And I got a velvet lion suit with a flexible tail and a silk mane. Cowardly, yes, but not Kmart.

Dad's costume was the best. Grandma ran it up from silver foil. He found a metal worker to do Tin Man's head.

"Dad, we could have saved a lot of trouble. We could go as ourselves, then pick costumes out of Lady Christobel's trunk," I told him.

"English costumes?" Dad said. "I don't think so. We're Americans. *The Wizard of Oz* is an American story, by an Illinois guy."

"Okay, Dad," I said. "Try to keep calm."

"Besides," he said. "I have to be Tin Man."

※ ✳ ※

On the night of the party the three of us were down in the front hall, waiting for Uncle Paul. He was going to take Dad in the Audi convertible because Tin Man's head and funnel hat were too tall to fit in the Lincoln or Mom's Subaru. We were admiring ourselves. My nose was black patent leather. My ears perked. I could do practically anything with my tail.

Under her busted straw farmer hat, Mom had big scarecrow circles painted on her cheeks. Actual straw came out of her plaid flannel cuffs. Her overalls were taken in at the waist. She was an excellent Scarecrow.

Dad was the best and shiny as a chrome bumper. Under the pointy hat his mask fitted down over his whole head, with weird round eyes cut out of the tin and an eerie small mouth. Kind of a space-alien Tin Man.

A footstep sounded on the stairs above us. My ears lay back on my velvet head.

Holly.

I'd forgotten about Holly. But here she came down the stairs, except she was Dorothy. The one with the apron, the artificial pigtails, the bobby socks, the ruby slippers, red as her lips. She'd rifled through the costume closet of the high school drama department.

"Oh, honey," Scarecrow said, "you look darling."

Dorothy clicked her ruby slippers.

"You're not a sixth grader," said Cowardly Lion, bravely. "You can't go to this party."

"If happy little bluebirds fly beyond the rainbow, why, oh why, can't I?" Dorothy said. "Besides, you little creep, look what the invitation says."

Scarecrow was holding the invitation, and of course it said "The Magill family."

"Precisely," Grandma Magill said, coming in from the back way. Sort of Grandma Magill. But now she was wearing a giant pink net dress with skirts sweeping the floor. It was pretty tight on top, and she had on a crown studded with fake jewels— emeralds. She gripped a wand with a glitter star at the end of it.

Scarecrow stifled a scream.

"Mama," Tin Man said, muffled. "Who are you?"

"I'm Glinda the Good Witch, obviously," Grandma said. "Who did you think I was, Aunty Em?"

"*Witch*," Scarecrow whispered behind me. "Didn't I always tell you?"

Then Uncle Paul walked in the front door with

the car keys in his hand. He was wearing what he wears to costume parties: a Ralph Lauren double-breasted dinner jacket, a pleated Tom Ford shirt with black butterfly bow tie, and pants with a quiet stripe down the side. "Nobody ever questions a dinner jacket," he says.

But we stopped him dead in his tracks. We were all here but the flying monkeys. Dorothy clicked her slippers for him. Cowardly Lion did something with his tail. Tin Man stared unblinking. Glinda drew a bead on him with her wand.

"We're off to see the wizard," Scarecrow explained.

"Oh," Uncle Paul said. "Then I guess we better hit the yellow brick road."

The town hadn't seen traffic like this since the lockdown days last spring. It was start and stop with some limos. But finally we were out by the carriage lamps of the former Showalter place.

The press was on the lawn, aiming cameras at the glowing windows. People without invitations were being escorted off the premises by black-suited consular muscle.

The two guests waiting just ahead of us seemed to be President and Mrs. Abraham Lincoln. Honest

Abe wore a top hat and a shawl. Mrs. Lincoln, who was a little larger than life, wore a hoop skirt and a bonnet.

I didn't know them, but Scarecrow reached out and gave Mrs. Lincoln a boost on her hoopskirt. She jumped and turned around. "Is that you, Marjorie?" It was Mrs. Stanley, and Abe was Mr. Stanley. Together again.

The door closed behind them. When it opened again, Glinda took Uncle Paul's arm. Scarecrow took Tin Man's. Cowardly Lion muttered to Dorothy, "This is so not your party," and in we went.

There to greet us was the ugliest woman who ever lived. And it wasn't a mask. Scarecrow gasped.

She was a really tall woman in a towering white wig, and her left arm was in a sling. She had on a Bo Peep costume, low in front but flat. A flock of fake sheep grazed by her skirt. In her free hand was a shepherd's crook.

"How very good of you to come," Bo Peep boomed. "I am Horace Calthorpe. Excuse the sling. I hit a reef. And I always choose this Bo Peep costume, as I am rather the black sheep of the family, haw, haw. Do come in. My wife will be down directly."

Beyond Bo Peep the party swirled across the marble floors under the blazing chandelier. Waiters in powdered wigs circulated with trays of punch cups. An orchestra played for dancing in the living room.

"This doesn't look a thing like Kansas," Scarecrow said. "Does it look like Kansas to you?"

The whole sixth grade was there in a lot of Kmart costumes. Sienna Searcy's girls went by without Sienna. They were all princesses of some kind. There were a ton of zombies. Still, we were outnumbered by grown-ups. Coming in behind us was the Mayor of Chicago. The real one.

The crowds parted, and Hilary was sitting on a settee at the foot of the curving stairs. He was Tiny Tim with an antique padded crutch. Next to him sat a ballerina, the number one swan from *Swan Lake*. Feathered headdress, black glitter eyes, mile-long legs in toe shoes.

Tiny Tim was saying to her, "Sit up, Esther. Be as tall as you can be."

I dragged Dorothy over to introduce her. But here came Lynn with two plates of food. She teetered in high-heeled shoes that buttoned up into her black skirt. She was wearing a tacky hat.

"Who are you?" we said.

"Mary Poppins," Lynn said. "I found this outfit upstairs. It wasn't in a trunk. I think Hilary's actual nanny wore it." In heels she was taller than I was. She was gaining on me. "I had to keep it simple," she said, "and I couldn't manage the umbrella. I have to feed these two. He can't walk in that cast. She can't walk in those toe shoes. They're both dead weight."

But now Dorothy was pulling me toward the dance floor. "I can't dance in these paws," I whined. "I can't dance at all."

"Hashtag you can't do anything," Dorothy said.

But I found Uncle Paul and handed her over.

It was mostly a dancing party. Tin Man and Scarecrow swooped around like they do in front of the tree at Christmas. And the Lincolns, together again. And here's a sight burned into my brain for all time: Grandma Glinda Good Witch doing a two-step with Bo Peep.

A gong sounded from high in the house. We all headed for the front hall. A consular servant in a powdered wig stood halfway up the stairs. "Ladies and gentlemen, pray silence for the entrance of your hostess, Lady Christobel, as Cleopatra, Queen of

Egypt and Serpent of the Nile, with all her retinue."

Another gong, and there was Lady Christobel at the top of the stairs with eyes like Esther's and a cobra crown. She was covered with jewels that looked real and held up a fake snake that looked way too real.

"There's Mummy with her asp in a basket!" piped Tiny Tim at the top of his little lungs.

Everybody cheered. After all, she looked every inch a queen, but then she's ninety-first in line. She nodded down pleasantly and waved her snake.

A servant woman attended her, wafting a big feathered fan to keep off the flies of ancient Egypt. The servant woman wasn't bad either, with bracelets up her arms and a wig cut low across her painted eyes. She made several Egyptian gestures.

"Who is it?" I muttered to Mary Poppins.

"I only know because I saw her getting made up," Mary Poppins said.

"Who?"

"Guess."

But I couldn't.

Cleopatra and her retinue started down the stairs. Her throne was borne aloft by two gigantic Egyptian strongmen. Their costumes were skimpy.

I mean skimpy. And the thongs on their sandals wound up to their massive knees. Their headdresses were higher than the feathered fan. I looked again, and one of them was Reginald. I looked one more time, and the other one was Andy. Westside Elementary's Andy, the guard who faints at needles. He seemed to be okay with Cleopatra's asp.

Down the curving stairs they carried Cleopatra into the midst of her loyal subjects. At the bottom her ancient Egyptian muscle helped her off her throne, and her handmaiden dropped a final curtsy. Several people dropped curtsies just to be on the safe side. And I'll say this about Lady Christobel as Cleopatra. She made a much better-looking woman than Lord Horace did.

I finally saw up close who her handmaiden was. It was Ms. Roebuck.

Later on, I caught another glimpse of Ms. Roebuck. She was on the dance floor, turning slowly in Reginald's arms.

"It could work," said a voice near my velvet ear. "Reginald and Ms. Roebuck. Why not?" said Mary Poppins. "And by the way, I'm going back to Lynette. I was never really a Lynn. And 'Lady Lynette' sounds better."

"And you'll be Lady Lynette because . . ."

"I'll be marrying Hilary."

"Does Hilary know?"

"He'll know when he needs to know," said Mary Poppins.

There's a cozy study off the living room, tucked under the curving stairs. It may have been Mr. Bob Showalter's man cave. Now portraits hang in there of all the Harewood family members the Calthorpes have married.

Tin Man sat on a sofa, looking into a fire snapping on the hearth. Cowardly Lion sat in a chair. Dorothy had danced Uncle Paul into the room, sharp in his dinner jacket.

"What are you guys doing?" he said, settling on the sofa.

"Taking a breather," Cowardly Lion said. "This partying is hard work."

"Be glad you're not Bo Peep," Uncle Paul said. "He's having to do it all in high heels."

"It's a great party, though. Right?" I figured Uncle Paul had been to enough parties to know.

"I can truly say I've never been to one like it," he said, "and everybody's here."

"Funny you should say that, Uncle Paul. I think Mr. McLeod's here. I think I saw him."

Uncle Paul smacked his forehead. "Nooo," he said.

"I think it was him." I scratched my patent-leather nose.

"I'll go out the back way," Uncle Paul said, and elbowed Tin Man. "Hey, Tin Man, you ready to call it a night?"

"How come you don't even want to see Mr. McLeod?" Cowardly Lion asked.

"Because I might weaken," Uncle Paul said. "After all, I'm passing up the greatest guy I'll ever meet, and I'm not going to feel like this about anybody else."

"Right," said the lion. "And I've looked ahead— I'm beginning to do that. Lynette Stanley's been doing it for years. Anyway, I've looked ahead, and you know what I see?"

"I don't," Uncle Paul said. "And it's a little hard to take you seriously since you look like a big stuffed toy."

"Well, do your best, Uncle Paul. Because Mr. McLeod's going to be deployed, sooner or later. Right? The National Guard's going to send him—"

"Yes," Uncle Paul said. "Get to the point, Lion."

"After it's over, he's going to need somebody to come home to. That's the point."

Uncle Paul looked away from the fire.

"And it ought to be you," said the lion.

Uncle Paul said, "Archer, don't con—"

"Yes, it ought to be you," said Tin Man, and took off his head. It was Mr. McLeod.

25

Uncle Paul and Mr. McLeod were married on a Saturday that next June.

Sixth grade was long over by then, even with the extra week of testing. Now we were twelve, or as Sienna Searcy said, virtually thirteen. Hilary had been out of his cast since Christmas, but Reginald was still providing muscle. And the high school let Holly attend graduation even though she'd blown up the chem lab. She was waitlisted for three colleges.

One Friday I was up in Mom's office. We were expecting Uncle Paul and Mr. McLeod for dinner. Garlic simmered up through the house. Dad was cooking. Things were fine. Then Holly blew in. She was wearing her CONFORMITY KILLS T-shirt. She and Janie Clarkson always wear them on the same day.

She pointed me to the far end of the sofa and flopped down. She had a problem. "If there's no bride in this wedding, how am I going to be bridesmaid? And I have to know like yesterday, because I'll need a dress. And I can't look thrown together."

"Honey," Mom said.

"Here's how I see it," Holly said. "If one of them proposed to the other, then the one proposed to is the bride, right?"

"No," Mom said. "Not right. Wrong, in so many ways, on so many levels."

Holly slumped. "So what kind of a wedding are we talking about here?"

Mom searched the ceiling in that way of hers. "At first Paul and Ed were talking about just going to a municipal office in Chicago, tying the knot with a cleaning lady for witness, then cutting out for a weekend at Lake Geneva."

Holly fidgeted.

"Then they were talking about booking Wrigley Field on an away day for the Cubs," Mom said. "Then they talked about the arboretum. Now I don't know what they're going to do. But don't worry about a dress, honey. You're in luck. I was bridesmaid for Mrs. Stanley. Oh golly, when was it? Twenty years ago. And I've saved the dress. Seafoam green with matching sash and a sweetheart neckline. I even have the shoes."

Holly gagged. She never gets Mom's quirky humor.

"I didn't want to do this," Holly said. "But you force my hand." She stood, eyes closed. "I'll have to take this problem to Grandma Magill." Then she left, eyes shut all the way to the door.

Silence fell behind her, and it felt good.

"Grandma Magill?" I said. "Does Grandma even know there can be weddings without brides?"

"I don't know," Mom said. "I just don't know."

"I mean, it can get complicated," I said. "Can there be a bachelor party when they're both bachelors?"

But Mom just sat at her desk with her eyes shut. It took me a while, but I finally saw she was being Holly.

Then we were all down in the kitchen. Dad was slicing roasted meat into a big pot of white beans.

Uncle Paul was thickening some tomato sauce. Mr. McLeod was chopping onions. Mom was tossing a salad. It was fine—a nice evening.

Then Grandma came in through the back door. She was in one of her League of Women Voters pantsuits. Holly followed.

Grandma made straight for the stove. "Did you soak those white beans overnight?" she asked.

"Yes, Mama," Dad said.

"Is that pork cooked through?" Grandma inquired.

"It fell off the bone, Mama."

"And you didn't add lamb, I hope. Your dad never liked lamb."

"Just a little hard Italian sausage," Dad said.

Dad was going to be cooking for another hour, but this isn't about what we'd be eating that night.

Grandma turned in the room.

"Grandma, I'd like you to meet Mr. McLeod," I said. She wouldn't have met him at Lady Christobel's party.

"Mr. McLeod, this is my grandma, Mrs. Magill."

"How do you do, ma'am," he said.

"You're quite a nice-looking young man, aren't you?" Grandma observed.

"Thank you, ma'am."

"Nobody ever tells me anything, so I have to rely on this girl for my information." She pointed back at Holly. "And when you hear it from Holly, it's all about Holly."

Even Holly had to agree with that.

"As far as I can tell," Grandma said past Uncle Paul, "you want to marry Paul Archer."

"I do," Mr. McLeod said. "I mean, that's my intention, ma'am."

Grandma looked over her glasses. "And what arrangements have you made for this event?"

"We haven't—"

"What man could ever plan a wedding, let alone his own?" Grandma said. "You will have to leave the arrangements to me. I will enlist my friend Lucille Ridgley. She owes me one. It will be a very simple wedding. Just a gathering of friends. No fuss. It won't even require a rehearsal. A porch wedding, as it's summer. My porch."

The League of Women Voters had made Grandma their President for Life, and you can see why.

"Another matter," she said. "I do not know your spiritual beliefs, and don't tell me. But I won't have a Justice of the Peace conducting the ceremony. It will have to be—"

"Me," Dad said from the stove.

We all looked. Grandma blinked.

"I'm a registered Marriage Officiant. I went online, paid the fifteen bucks, and got ordained," Dad said. "So I can marry them."

Dad looked at Uncle Paul and Mr. McLeod. "If that's okay with you guys," he said. "I can do the cake too."

It was okay with them, but surprising.

And if Dad was going to officiate, did that move me up to best man? My heart kind of stopped. I looked at Uncle Paul and pointed to myself. He nodded.

But wait. What about Mr. McLeod? Could I be *his* best man too, like double-duty? I looked at him and pointed to myself again. He nodded and turned up both thumbs.

Grandma was getting ready to go.

"Stay for dinner, Mama," Dad said.

"Dinner? With all I have to do?" she said. "The lists, the flowers, the music. Marjorie," she called out to Mom, "you will need to take charge of the guest book and make sure everybody signs. It's just such details as these that can make or break a wedding."

She was almost out the door. But she turned back.

"I was married in a meadow, you know. Barefoot in a field of daisies, and I'd ironed my hair. I wore flowers in it. Real ones."

Then she was gone, out into the evening.

There wasn't a bachelor party, but a mammoth reception was coming because a hundred and twenty-five chairs were unfolded on the lawn. Dad, who was officiating, was practically a dot in the distance. There aren't any small weddings. There's always fuss.

We needed a battalion of ushers to get everybody sitting down: Mr. McLeod's National Guardsmen and Uncle Paul's Sigma Nu brothers.

Up on the porch a string quartet was working through "You Are the Wind Beneath My Wings."

Just inside the front door at Grandma's house we waited, the best man and the grooms.

And Holly.

Yes, Holly. It was just easier to let her be bridesmaid even though there wasn't a bride. She waited at the front door ahead of us, fidgeting with a bunch of glads from Grandma's garden.

I told you about my suit—Ralph Lauren, right?

Dark blue in a summer weight and a lot like Uncle Paul's. Cuffed pants. We got matching ties. My tie was long on me, but I'll get there.

Mr. McLeod was in his dress uniform. Knife creases in his pants, shoes like mirrors, cap in the crook of his arm. Look at that haircut. And wait till the sunlight hits those brass buttons.

Out on the porch the string quartet waited, holding their bows. As best man, I asked Uncle Paul and Mr. McLeod if they were ready, and they said they were. They were going to walk side by side, down the aisle to Dad. Two guys already together. And I'd come along behind.

"Let's do it," I said, and told Holly to tell the quartet to hit it. She did, and they struck up "America the Beautiful" in march time. She pushed through the screen door and walked out across the porch.

With her new dress she had on Dorothy's slippers from the party last fall. At the top of the porch stairs she clicked her ruby heels and started down into the waiting crowd.

She got her moment. She always does.

Then we set off across the porch. "Wow," said one of the string quartet.

We took our time. It was a great, dappled day. Everybody's phone was out. A flash or two came from the trees across the street. Lady Christobel was there in an English hat and with her the Hon. Hilary and Lord Horace. The anchorwoman of the ABC affiliate had crashed the party, but the ushers knew her from the evening news and let her stay. Everybody was there. All the troops, including Natalie Schuster.

Dad kept getting bigger and closer behind a spray of flowers at his podium. He was wearing an old Palm Beach summer coat of Grandpa's, and a tie. Nobody had ever seen him outdoors without a baseball cap before.

We drew up.

"Who gives this man to this man?" he asked, about Uncle Paul.

"I do." Mom stood up from the front row. "His sister."

"Okay. Thanks, honey," Dad said. "Who gives this man to this man?" he asked, about Mr. McLeod.

"I do," said Mrs. Stanley, "his critic teacher." She stood up from her seat between Mr. Stanley and Lynette.

"So do I," said Mrs. Velma Dempsey, rising out of

a row farther back, "as principal of Westside Elementary."

"So do we," said all the troops, standing up all over the lawn.

Dad looked around to see if anybody else wanted to give Mr. McLeod away. Then he went on. I forget the order of things after that.

Uncle Paul and Mr. McLeod exchanged rings. I told Uncle Paul I'd had to be ring bearer in the last wedding, and I couldn't go through that again. They carried the rings in their own pockets.

"Put that ring on that man's hand," Dad said, twice. Then he covered their hands with his. A pile of big hands.

They exchanged vows. They promised to love and honor and not necessarily obey each other.

Then by the powers vested in him by Cook County and the State of Illinois, Dad pronounced them married.

"Be there together
Through any weather,"
he told them.
"Though the world fall apart,
Stand heart-to-heart."
And they said they would.

"Repeat after me," Dad said: "We believe in the Cubs and each other."

And they did.

"You may kiss the groom," Dad said. "You may kiss the groom."

26

Like I said. There's some cake left.

The reception's been such a great party that Grandma Magill's porch is still a big throng of people. Lynette and Mr. and Mrs. Stanley just left. Lynette had scored a new outfit for the occasion. I didn't understand it, but it really annoyed Natalie all the way across the porch.

I guess Lynette and I have made some progress over these six years. We started our last wedding under the porch, not on it. Of course we were just kids then. And you know Lynette; she looks ahead, not back.

Which brings up Hilary Evelyn. Reginald just came to pick up the three Calthorpes in a limo from the consulate. The limo's just pulling away from the kerb.

And the grooms have been gone twenty minutes. Everybody thought they'd blast off in Uncle Paul's Audi. Instead, Dad pulled Mr. McLeod's beat-up Kia around to the front of Grandma's house, and they tooled away in that before anybody noticed. Dad had it worked out. Dad was there.

I was willing to let them go. I'd done my best man duties, and I'd be seeing them for all the years to come. But they found me over in my corner of the porch. Uncle Paul handed me something. A little black velvet box, and inside it a pair of gold cuff links. Totally grown-up.

"Are these for Dad?" I said. "Because he doesn't—"

"They're for you. Best men get presents from the grooms," Uncle Paul said. "Besides, you helped all this happen, man. You helped us happen."

Me?

Man.

Now I couldn't see the box. It was blurry or something.

I couldn't see the box, but I could see me shooting my cuffs to show off my gold cuff links at all the big occasions of my life unfolding in the future.

Now they were going. We made a pile of hands, the three of us, and their new rings gleamed bright as Mr. McLeod's buttons.

"One more thing," he said. "No more Mr. McLeod. I'm your uncle now."

I hadn't thought that far. You know how I am. I take my sweet time.

"I married your uncle, so I'm your other uncle. And I've never had a nephew. You'll have to show me the ropes."

Mr. McLeod never had a niece either. But, hey, why spoil the moment?

Then my uncles turned to go, off into the blurry afternoon, looking good. They seemed to mingle with the guests on the lawn, but they were working their way to the Kia, Uncle Paul and Mr. McLeod. He's still Mr. McLeod on this page. I can't turn on a dime. But I'll get there. I got this far.

The string quartet was playing dance tunes now, so Mom was looking around for Dad.

Dad

Uncle Paul

Mr. McLeod

The three I wanted to be.

And Grandpa, still there in our hearts, except for about a tablespoon of him in Wrigley Field.